A Candlelight Ecstasy Classic Romance

**"WHAT DO YOU THINK YOU'RE DOING?"
ANNE NEARLY CHOKED ON THE WORDS.**

Jud released her and moved away, turning his back to her as he walked around the desk. "I told you before. I expect all the fringe benefits the old man had. Were you naive enough to think that your—how should I say it—devotion to my father had gone unnoticed? Or that the word hadn't spread?"

Anne's mind filled with horror. What was he saying? Surely no one in their right mind would think that she and her stepfather were . . . "What do you mean? Exactly what are you accusing me of?"

"Come off it, Anne. It's been whispered about for some time now. It's nothing very new or novel. An older man seeking the virility of his youth with a young woman. Or, in this case, you endeavoring to show your gratitude in whatever way he wished. Or did you convince yourself you were in love with him?"

Be sure to read this month's other
CANDLELIGHT ECSTASY CLASSIC ROMANCE . . .

GENTLE PIRATE, *Jayne Castle*

Next month in the
CANDLELIGHT ECSTASY CLASSIC ROMANCE
publishing program, don't miss . . .

THE PASSIONATE TOUCH, *Bonnie Drake*
ONLY THE PRESENT, *Noelle Berry McCue*

CANDLELIGHT ECSTASY ROMANCES®

THE TAWNY GOLD MAN

Amii Lorin

A CANDLELIGHT ECSTASY CLASSIC ROMANCE

A CANDLELIGHT ECSTASY CLASSIC ROMANCE
Published by
Dell Publishing Co., Inc.
1 Dag Hammarskjold Plaza
New York, New York 10017

Dell ® TM 681510, Dell Publishing Co., Inc.

A Candlelight Ecstasy Classic Romance

Candlelight Ecstasy Romance®, 1,203,540, is a registered trademark of Dell Publishing Co., Inc., New York, New York.

ISBN: 0-440-18978-0

Printed in the United States of America

One Previous Edition

August 1986

10 9 8 7 6 5 4 3 2 1

WFH

To Our Readers:

By popular demand, we are happy to announce that we will be bringing you two Candlelight Ecstasy Classic Romances every month.

In the upcoming months, your favorite authors and their earlier best-selling Candlelight Ecstasy Romances will be available once again.

As always, we will continue to present the distinctive, sensuous love stories that you have come to expect only from Ecstasy and also the very finest work from new authors of contemporary romantic fiction.

Your suggestions and comments are always welcome. Please write to us at the address below.

Sincerely,

The Editors
Candlelight Romances
1 Dag Hammarskjold Plaza
New York, New York 10017

CHAPTER

1

~~~~

"In the name of the Father, the Son, and the Holy Spirit. Amen."

The solemnly intoned benediction seemed to hang like a pall on the chill March air long seconds after the pastor closed his prayer book. A muffled sob shattered the silence, and, as if the cry had been a signal, the large crowd around the grave site began to move in a slow, unsure manner.

Some distance off to one side, in a small, sparse stand of trees, a tall man stood, unobserved by the group of mourners. Hands thrust inside the deep pockets of a hip-length sheepskin jacket, broad shoulders hunched, wide collar flipped up against the cold, damp air, all that was visible of his head and face was a shock of sun-gold hair and a pair of amber eyes, narrowed and partially concealed by long, thick, dark-brown lashes. At the moment, the eyes were riveted on the flower-draped brass casket suspended over the open grave.

The figure remained still as a statue, but the eyes, cold and unemotional, shifted to the source of the low sobs. A small fair-haired woman, dressed entirely in black, stood unsteadily, supported on both sides by two tall, slender, fair-haired young men who wore the same face. The cold eyes flashed for an instant with cynicism, gone as fast as it came, then moved on to rest on the face of a younger woman, also dressed in black, standing close to the one of the young men. There was an oddly protective attitude in her stance, although she was much smaller than the man. The amber eyes grew stormy as they studied the small, pale, wistfully lovely face, the soft, pure lines set in fierce determination. The lids dropped, and the eyes again became clear and cold and moved on to briefly scan the crowd before once again coming to rest on the coffin, gleaming dully in the gray, overcast morning light.

"I loved you, you old bastard."

The softly muttered words bounced off the warm fleece of the collar; then the man turned sharply and strode through the trees to the road some yards away and a low, black Firebird parked to the side.

Anne rested her head against the plush upholstery of the limousine, eyes closed. She was tired and the day wasn't half over. There would be a lot of people coming back to the house and she'd have to act as hostess, as her mother obviously wasn't up to it. The soft weeping coming from the seat in front of her gave evidence of that. Not for the first time Anne wished she'd known her father, for she surely must have inherited his character. For although except for hair color she resembled her small, fragile mother, beyond the surface features there was very little comparison. Her mother was gentle natured but had always been high strung and of delicate health, whereas Anne had enormous stamina and strength for such a small woman. About the only thing she and her mother shared by way of emotions was the gentle nature. Ann was a pushover for any hard-luck or sob

6

story and had been taken in by and involved with so many of her friends' problems she had finally had to harden her heart in self-defense.

Taking advantage of the drive back to the house to relax, Anne's mind was going over what still had to be gotten through that day when a disturbing thought pushed its way forward: He didn't even come to his father's funeral. Her head moved restlessly; her soft lips tightened bitterly. For days now, ever since her stepfather's death, she had managed to push away all thoughts of her stepbrother, but even so she had felt sure he would be at the funeral. Of course it had been ten years, but still, he had been notified and the least he could do . . . She felt the car turn into the driveway and, opening her eyes, sat up straight, pushing the disquieting thoughts away.

During the next two hours Anne was kept too busy to do any deep thinking, but still her eyes went to the door each time the housekeeper opened it to admit yet another friend offering condolences.

When finally the door was closed after the last well-wisher, Anne sighed deeply before squaring her shoulders and walking to the door of the library. With her hand on the knob she paused, her gaze moving slowly around the large, old-fashioned foyer. The woodwork was dark, gleaming in the light of the chandelier that hung from the middle of the ceiling. The furnishings could only be described as heavy and ornate. Anne didn't really care too much for the house, yet it had been the only home she'd ever known, as Judson Cammeron, Sr., had been the only father she'd ever known. Sighing again, she turned the knob and entered the room.

Mr. Slonne, the family attorney, sat dwarfed behind her stepfather's massive oak desk, hands folded on the blotter in front of him. He was speaking quietly to her mother, who was sitting in a chair alongside the desk. As Anne gently closed the door he glanced up and asked, "Everyone gone?"

Smiling faintly, Anne nodded and moved to the chair placed at the other side of the desk. As she sat down, her eyes scanned her mother's face.

"How are you feeling now, Mother?"

Margaret Cammeron smiled wanly at her daughter, her eyes misty. "Better, dear." Her tremulous voice had a lost, childlike note. "I don't know how I'd have managed to get through this without you and your brothers." Her breath caught and her hand reached out for, and was grasped by, that of her son who leaped from his chair and came to stand beside hers.

"Well, you don't have to get through anything without us, ever." Anne spoke bracingly, her eyes going to first one, then another, set of matching blue eyes, in the faces of her identical-twin half brothers.

Like a small mother hen, Anne was proud of her younger brothers. Usually carefree and unhampered by responsibility, due to too little discipline and too much indulgence Anne admitted ruefully, that their conduct the last few days had been faultless. At twenty-one and in their last year of college, Troy and Todd Cammeron had never done a full day's serious work. They had inherited their mother's sweet nature and their father's quick temper, but little of his iron will and tenacity. They were good-looking and well-liked and too busy having a good time to worry about the future. Their father was rich and they had known they would go to work in his business when they left school. Meanwhile they had been busy with girls and cars and girls and fun and girls. Their father's sudden death had shocked them, as it had everyone, but they had rallied well in support of their mother. Although only four years their senior, Anne also admitted she

8

had had as much of a hand, if not more, in their spoiling as anyone.

Mr. Slonne glanced at his watch then cleared his throat discreetly. "I think we had better begin, Mrs. Cammeron. The time stated was two o'clock and as it is now two-fifteen I—"

He stopped, startled, as the library door was thrust open and Anne felt the breath catch in her throat as her stepbrother walked briskly into the room. He paused, his eyes making a circuit of the room, then proceeded to her mother.

"Sorry I'm late, Margaret, I stopped for something to eat and the service was lousy."

Anne shivered at his tone. So unfeeling, so cold, could this hard-eyed man be her stepbrother?

Margaret raised astonished eyes to his face, murmuring jerkily, "That—that's all right, Jud. But you—you should have come home to eat."

His smile was a mere twist of the lips before his head lifted to turn from one then the other twin, standing on either side of her chair.

"Troy, Todd, still the same bookends, I see."

Their faces wore the same strained expressions, but both stretched out hands to grasp the one he had extended. He nodded to the lawyer, murmured "Mr. Slonne" then turned to Anne. She felt a small flutter in her chest as he walked to the chair next to hers.

"Anne."

His tone was low, but so coolly impersonal that Anne again felt a shiver go through her. Was it possible for a man to change so much in ten years? Apparently it was, for the proof of it was sitting next to her.

He had left home a charming, laughing, teasing young man and had walked through that door a few minutes ago with the lazy confidence of a proud, tawny lion. And tawny was the only way to describe him. The fair hair of ten years ago had darkened to a sun gold, and his skin was a burnished bronze. His features hadn't changed, of course, but had matured, sharpened. The broad forehead now held several creases as did the corners of his eyes. The long nose that had been perfectly straight now sported a bump, evidence of a break surgically corrected. The once firm jawline now looked as if it had been cut from granite. The well-shaped mouth now seemed to be permanently cast in a mocking slant. And the once laughing amber eyes arched over by sun-bleached brows now held the mysterious, wary glow of the jungle cat. Incredibly he seemed to have grown a few inches and gained about thirty pounds and he looked big and powerful and very, very dangerous.

With a feeling of real grief Anne felt a small light go out inside for the death of the laughing, teasing Jud Cammeron she'd known ten years before.

Mr. Slonne lifted the papers that had been lying on the desk and with a sharp movement Jud lifted his hand.

"If you'll be patient just a few more minutes, Mrs. Davis is bringing me something to drink." Then he turned to Margaret. "I hope you don't mind."

Her still lovely face flushed, Margaret whispered, "No—no, of course not."

At that moment the library door opened and the housekeeper, her face set in rigid lines of disapproval, entered the room carrying a tray bearing a coffeepot, cups, sugar bowl, and creamer. Mrs. Davis had been with the Cammerons only six years and she obviously looked on this new arrival as an interloper. Placing the tray, none too gently, on a small table beside Jud's chair, she turned on her heel and marched out of the room. Hearing him laugh softly, Anne thought

10

in amazement, *He's enjoying her discomfort. No, he's enjoying the discomfort of all of us.* And for the third time she felt a shiver run through her body.

Mr. Slonne waited patiently while Jud filled his cup and added cream. Then he began reading. The atmosphere in the room grew chill then cold as he read on. Anne, her hands gripping the arms of her chair, couldn't believe her ears. Her mother's face was white with shock. The twins wore like expressions of incredulity. Jud sat calmly sipping his coffee, his eyes cold and flat as a stone and his face a mask. When the lawyer's voice finally ground to a halt, the room was in absolute silence. After a few long, nerve-racking minutes Jud's unemotional voice broke the silence.

"Well, then, it seems, in effect, he's left it all to me."

"Precisely."

Mr. Slonne's clipped corroboration brought the rest of them out of their trance.

"I—I don't understand," Margaret wailed.

Mr. Slonne hastened to reassure her. "There is no need for concern, Mrs. Cammeron, you've been well provided for. Indeed you've all been well provided for. It is just that Mr. Cammeron, young Mr. Cammeron, will have control of the purse strings, so to speak. In effect, he will be taking over where your husband left off."

"You mean I'll have to ask Jud for everything?" she cried.

Before Mr. Slonne could answer, Jud rapped. "Did you have to ask the old man for everything?"

Margaret winced at the term "old man," then answered wildly. "But you've been away for ten years. Not once have you written or called. It was as if

11

you'd died. He never mentioned your name after you left this house. Why should he do this?"

Jud's eyes went slowly from face to face, reading the same question in all but Mr. Slonne's. Then with cool deliberation he said, "Maybe because the business that made him so wealthy was started mainly with Carmichael money. My mother's father's money. Maybe because he was afraid there was no one here who could handle it. And just maybe because he trusted me. Even after ten years."

He paused as if expecting a protest, and when there was none he continued. "Don't concern yourself, Margaret. You're to go on as you always have. I will question no expenditures except exceedingly large ones. This house is as much your home as it ever was, I have no intention of interfering with its running."

"You are going to live here?" Dismayed astonishment tinged Margaret's tone and one not-quite-white eyebrow arched sardonically.

"Of course. At least for the next few months. As you said, I've been away for a long time. I'll have to familarize myself with the company, its management. Perhaps make a few changes."

Anne didn't like the ominous sound of his tone or the significance of his last words. Incautiously she snapped, "What changes?"

She realized her mistake as he turned slowly to face her. He didn't bother to answer her, he didn't have to. His eyebrows arched exceedingly high, the mocking slant of his hard mouth said it all loud and clear: *Who the hell are you to question me?* Anne felt her cheeks grow warm, heard him laugh softly when her eyes shied away from his intent amber stare.

"Now, then." The abrupt change in his tone startled Anne so much she actually flinched. "Mr.

12

Slonne, thank you for your time and your assistance, you will be hearing from me soon." The lawyer was ushered politely, but firmly, out of the room. Margaret was next. In tones soothing but unyielding, Jud saw her to the door with the opinion that she should rest for at least an hour or so.

When Jud turned back to face her and her brothers, Anne felt her palms grow moist, her heart skip a beat. In no way did this man resemble the Jud she remembered. The Jud she had known ten years ago, had had laughing eyes and a teasing voice. This man had neither. His eyes were alert and wary, and his voice, so far, was abrupt and sarcastic. This man was a stranger with a hard, dangerous look that spoke of ruthlessness.

"Now, you three," Jud said coolly. "I think we had better have a small conclave, set down the ground rules as it were."

Troy was the first one to speak. "What do you mean ground rules? And who the hell are you to lay down rules anyway?"

"I should think the answer to that would be obvious, even to you, Troy." Completely unruffled, Jud moved around the desk, lazily lowering himself into his father's chair.

"Sit down," he snapped. "This may take longer then I thought."

"I prefer to stand."

"So do I," Todd added.

The twins then began to speak almost simultaneously. Beginning to feel shaky with the premonition of what was coming, Anne was only too happy to sink into the chair she had so recently vacated. Jud pinned her there with a cold stare.

"I'll get to you shortly."

He turned the stare to the twins and his voice took

on the bite of a January midnight. "I will tell you exactly who I am. As our father saw fit to leave me in control, from now on I'm the boss. And there are going to be a lot of changes made, starting with you two earning your keep."

"What do you mean?"

"In what way?"

He silenced them with a sharp, slicing move of his hand.

"From today on every free day you have, except Sundays, will be spent at the mill learning the textile business from the ground up, starting with the upcoming Easter vacation."

"But we have plans made to go to Lauderdale at Easter," Troy exclaimed angrily.

"*Had* plans," Jud stated flatly. "There will be no romping on the sands for you two this year."

"We're over twenty-one," Todd sneered. "You can't make us do anything.

"Can't I?"

Anne felt her mouth go dry at the silky soft tone. Her eyes shifted to the twins' faces as Jud continued.

"Perhaps not. But I can stop your allowances. I can neglect to pay your school fees for the final term. I can demand board payment for living in this house—my house."

White-faced, Troy cried, "We still have our income from the business."

"Wrong," Jud said coldly. "You heard the terms of the old man's will. Unless I choose to sign a release, every penny of that income goes into a trust fund until you are twenty-five. I'm the only one who can draw on that fund for your maintenance. Now, unless you want to be cut off without a penny for the next four years, when I say jump, the only question I want from either of you is: How high?"

Anne closed her eyes to shut out the glazed expression of shocked disbelief on her brothers' faces. With a tingling shiver she heard Jud coolly dismiss them with the advice they attend their mother, then her eyes flew open at his crisp "Now you."

"You can't frighten me, Jud. You have no control over me whatever. I have simply to pack my things and walk out of this house to be away from your—control."

Anne felt an angry flush of color flare in her face as he studied her with amused insolence, his eyes seeming to strip her of every stitch of clothing she was wearing.

"That's exactly right," he finally replied silkily. "But you won't. The old man was no fool. His plan was beautifully simple. He knew full well the sons of his second marriage were incapable of taking over, while at the same time he wanted to insure their future, so he split up forty-five percent of the company stock between them but left me in control of the actual capital. At the same time he knew I could handle the business and the twins, and that I would. But he wanted a check rein on me, too, so he only left me forty-five percent. That leaves you, right in the middle, with the other ten percent."

"To do with as I please," she inserted warningly.

"But of course," he countered smoothly. "But as I said, the old man was no fool. He was reasonably sure you would not surrender your share to me, thus giving me full control. On the other hand he could also feel reasonably sure you would not throw in with the twins, as you are as aware as he was that they would probably run the company right into the ground. Does it give you a feeling of power, Anne?"

"You can't be sure I won't sell or give my share to

15

Troy and Todd." Very angry now, she lashed out at him blindly. Everything he'd said was true, and she hated his cool smugness.

"Right again," he mocked. "But, like the old man, I am reasonably certain, and being so, I'll call the shots. And I'll give you one warning: If you decide you can't hack it, and to hurt me you sign over to the twins, I'll ruin them—and I can, easily."

Wetting her lips she stared at him in disbelief. He meant it.

"But you'd be destroying your own interests as well."

Mocking smile deepening, he shrugged carelessly. "I'll admit that I want it, but I don't need it to survive. The twins do. And don't, for one moment, deceive yourself into thinking I won't do it. I will."

She believed him. He wasn't just bluffing or trying to scare her, though he did. He meant it. Confused, frightened for her brothers, she cried. "Why are you taking this position? Do you hate us all so much?"

"Hate? The twins?" Again the brows rose in exaggerated surprise. "You forget, the twins are my brothers too. I'll be the making of them."

The fact did not escape her that he referred to Troy and Todd only. Shocked by a pain she had thought long dead, she argued. "You're being too hard on them."

"Hard?" He gave a short bark of laughter, shaking his head. "You call it hard to expect them to learn a business they have almost a half interest in? Good grief, girl, they are twenty-one years old and have never done a full day's work. Do you know how old I was when I went to work for my father?"

Subdued by his sudden anger, Anne shook her head dumbly.

"I was fourteen. Fourteen." His tone hardened on

16

the repeated word. "And how old were you? Don't answer, I know. You've had almost sole care of those two ever since you were six. You've cared for, protected, and played general guard dog to them from the time they could say your name. How old were you when you went to work in the old man's office?"

"Eighteen."

"Eighteen," he repeated softly. "No carefree college days for Anne."

"I wasn't his daughter," she protested. "I never expected—"

"No, you weren't his daughter," he interrupted. "You were, for all intents and purposes, his slave."

"He was very good to me." She almost screamed at him.

"Why the hell shouldn't he have been?" he shouted. "You never made a move he disapproved of."

Anne drew deep breaths, forcing herself to calm down. This was proving nothing. Her voice more steady, she said quietly, "I won't argue anymore about this, Jud. If there is nothing else you want to discuss I'll go up to moth—"

"There is," he cut in firmly. "If you have any papers or anything else pertaining to the office here at home, I'd like you to get them together. My secretary will be in the office tomorrow and it will be easier for her if—"

Now it was Anne's turn to interrupt. Her voice hollow with shock, she cried, "Your secretary? But that's my office."

Even though his voice was bland, it chilled her.

"I don't need you in that office, Anne, that's what I pay my secretary for. So if there's anything here, collect it before tomorrow. Now if you'll excuse me, I have some phone calls to make."

Turning quickly, Anne left the room. She heard him dialing as she closed the door. Then she stood staring at her trembling hands. That easily, that coolly, she had been dismissed, not only from the room but from the office as well. Fighting tears, she ran upstairs to her bedroom. What was she supposed to do now?

CHAPTER

2

~~~

Anne paced the deep rose carpet in her lovely pink
and white bedroom, Jud's words still ringing in her
ears. If she wasn't to go to the office and he didn't
want her to move out of the house, what was she to
do? Get another job? Work for a rival company?
That didn't make much sense. Maybe he meant her
to stay at home, run the house, live the kind of life
her mother did. Women's clubs and bridge games and
shopping week in, week out. Anne shivered. She
would go out of her mind. Maybe if the twins were
still small enough to keep her running, but not now.
She was too used to the office. Tears trickling down
her face, she riled silently. Didn't he realize she
knew almost as much about the managerial end of
the business as his father had? She could be of help to
him while he was familiarizing himself with it. Why
had he turned her out? Did he hate her that much?

In frustration she flung herself onto the bed and
stared at the ceiling. He had changed so drastically.
Uninvited and unwelcome, a picture of him as he
was the last time she saw him formed in her mind.
How young she had been then. Young and naive and
so very much in love. Anne's face burned at the
memory of how very gullible she had been at fifteen.

* * *

It had been Jud's twenty-fifth birthday and Anne had waited with growing impatience for him to come home to dinner. She felt her spirits drop when her stepfather came home alone and when he told her mother that Jud would not be home for dinner as he had a date, her spirits sank completely.

The hours had seemed to drag endlessly as Anne, unable to sleep, sat in her room, ears strained for the sound of his car on the driveway. On the table beside her small bedroom chair lay a tiny birthday present, its fancy bow almost twice the size of the package. At intervals Anne touched the bow gently, lovingly. She had saved so long to buy this gift, had been so eager to give it to him. Eager and also a little nervous. It was not quite a year since she had first seen the brush-finished gold cufflinks and she had known at once she wanted to give them to him. At first she had thought of giving them to him at Christmas but she had not been able to save enough money. So she had taken the money she had and had talked to the store manager. He in turn had removed the links from the display window, put her name on them, and had set them aside for her. She had made the last payment on them the previous week. Now, staring at the small, wrapped box, she saw the mat surface of the gold ovals, could see the initials engraved on them. J.C.C. Judson Carmichael Cammeron. How she loved him. And how she prayed he'd like her offering.

The slam of the car door startled Anne out of a daze. The front door being closed brought her fully aware. She heard him come up the stairs, pass her door, and his own door close farther down the hall. What should she do? It was past two thirty. Would he be angry if she went to his room now? Should she wait until morning?

Anne hesitated long minutes. Then she thought fiercely, *No, it won't be the same. By morning his birthday will be truly over.* Without giving herself time to change her mind, she slipped out of her room and along the thickly carpeted hall on noiseless bare feet. She tapped on his door softly then held her breath. It seemed to take a very long time for him to open the door, but when she did she knew why at once. He had obviously just come out of the shower, as his hair was damp and he was wearing nothing except a mid-calf-length belted terry cloth robe. At the sight of him Anne felt her resolve weaken, but before she could utter an apology or whisper good night, he caught her hand and said with concern, "Anne! What is it? Is something wrong?"

Her voice pleading for understanding, Anne shook her head quickly and answered softly, "No, nothing. I'm—I'm sorry to disturb you. I'm silly. I wanted to give you your birthday present and I couldn't wait till morning."

Jud sighed, but his voice was gentle. "You're right; you are silly." He paused, then chided, "Well, where is this present you couldn't wait to give me?"

Flushing, Anne slid her hand into the pocket of the cotton housecoat she'd slipped the gift into before leaving her room. As she withdrew the gift, he gave a light tug on the hand he was still holding and murmured ruefully, "You had better come in. We don't want to wake the household for the event of giving and receiving one gift."

She stepped inside and he reached around her to close the door before taking the small package from the palm of her hand. Silently he removed the wrapping and silently he flipped the case open and stared a very long time at the cufflinks. When he raised his eyes to hers they were serious, questioning. Fear

21

gripped her and she blurted breathlessly, "Don't you like them, Jud?"

"Like them? Of course I like them, they're beautiful. But, chicken, they must have cost a bundle. Why?"

More nervous than before, Anne plucked at the button on her robe.

"I—I saw them in the window and—and I wanted to buy them for you."

"When was this?" he asked softly.

"Almost—not quite a year ago."

"And you've been saving all this time?" His voice was even softer now and Anne shivered. His tone—something—was making her feel funny.

"Are you angry with me, Jud?"

"Angry? With you? Oh, honey, I could never be really angry at you."

"I'm glad," she whispered. "I wanted to give them to you tonight so badly. I could have cried when you didn't come home for dinner."

His beautiful amber eyes seemed to flicker, grow shadowed and he carefully laid the jeweler's box on the night table by his bed, then brought his hand to her face. Again a tiny shiver went through her as his fingers lightly touched her skin. Now his voice was barely above a murmur. "And do I get a birthday kiss too?"

"Yes." A mere whisper broke from a suddenly tight throat.

His blond head descended and then she felt his lips touch hers lightly and tenderly. The pressure on her lips increased and then he groaned softly and pulled his head away with a muttered growl. "You had better get out of here, Anne."

She felt stricken, shattered, and as he turned away

she cried, without thinking, "Jud, please, I love you. What have I done wrong?"

He swung back, his eyes filled with pain.

"Wrong? Oh, chicken, you've done nothing wrong. Don't you see? Can't you tell? I want to kiss you properly and you're so young. Too young. I think you'd better get out of here before I hurt you."

His eyes burned into hers, and with a feeling of fierce elation she couldn't begin to understand running through her, she pleaded, "Oh, Jud, please don't make me go. Tell me, show me, what to do, please."

He moved closer to her, his eyes searching hers as if looking for answers. Again his hand touched her face lightly, then his forefinger brushed, almost roughly, across her lips. Her lips parted fractionally in automatic reaction and leaning closer he whispered, "Like that, honey." Again his finger brushed her mouth, this time the lower lip only, and she could hardly hear his murmured "Part your lips for me, Anne" before his lips were against hers. She obeyed him and felt a shock of mingled fear and joy rip through her as his mouth crushed hers. Never could she have imagined the riot of sensations that stormed her senses.

When his mouth left hers, she gave a low "no" in protest, and grasping her arm, he whispered, "Come."

He led her to the side of the bed, sat her down, then sat down beside her. Cupping her head in his hands he stared broodingly into her face a long time before saying quietly, "Sweetheart, if you're at all frightened, tell me now while I can still send you back to your room."

Her eyes clear, she faced him without fear. "I could never be afraid of you, Jud. How could I be? I told you. I love you."

"Yes, you told me," he groaned. Then he was on

23

his feet, moving away from her. "But, honey, I'm not talking about brother-sister love. You know the facts of life?"

She looked up indignantly at the sharp question. "Yes, of course I do."

His tone lost none of its sharpness. "Then you know what I want?"

Unable to voice the answer, Anne lowered her eyes, nodded her head.

"Honey, look at me."

Some of the edge had left his tone and in relief Anne looked up.

"Ever since the day you first came to this house, I loved you. Like a brother with a small sister, I loved you, wanted to protect you. A little over a year ago, some months after your fourteenth birthday, I began to feel different." Anne felt a pain twist at her heart and she would have cried out but he held up his hand to explain. "Suddenly one day I realized I did not love you as a brother loves a sister. I was in love with you, the way a man loves a woman." His eyes closed but not before Anne saw the pain in them.

"Jud." She made to get up and go to him.

"No." It was an order. Anne stayed where she was. His eyes were again open. His voice wracked with torment, he went on. "I don't know how. I don't know why. But, dear God, Anne, I love you and you are too young. Get out of here, chicken. Go back to your room while I can still let you go."

"No."

"Anne."

"No, Jud." She repeated firmly then more softly, "Jud, please. I don't want to go. I want to stay with you."

In three strides he was back beside her, his hands again cradling her head. "You are a small, beautiful

24

fool. And I will very likely squirm in hell, but, honey, I need you so, want you so."

This time when his mouth touched hers she needed no prompting. Eager to experience again that wild riot of sensations, her lips parted beneath his searching, hungry mouth. His hand dropped to her shoulders then moved down and over her back, drawing her slight, soft body against his large, hard one.

Slowly, reluctantly, his lips released hers, moved over her face and she felt her breath quicken as he dropped feather-light kisses across her cheeks, on her eyelids, and along the edge of her ear. Breathing stopped completely for a moment when his teeth nipped gently on her lobe and he whispered urgently, "Anne, I want you to touch me. Put your hands on my chest, inside the robe."

Her hands had been laying tightly clasped on her lap and at his words she relaxed them, brought them slowly up. Slowly, shyly, she parted the lapels of his robe, then placed her palms against his hair-roughened skin. Enjoying the feel of him, she grew braver and slid her hands across the broad expanse of his chest. He shuddered, then moaned deep in his throat when her fingertip brushed his nipple. Made still braver by his reaction to her touch, she whispered. "Do you like that, Jud?"

"Like it?" he husked. "Lord, sweetheart, I love the feel of your hands on me. I just hope you enjoy the feel of my touch half as much." His hands moved to the buttons of her robe, unfastening them quickly. His lips close to hers, he murmured, "I don't think we need all this material between us."

He slipped the robe off then gathered her close against him, his mouth driving her to the edge of delirium as he explored the hollow at the base of her throat. Anne stiffened with a gasp when his hand moved caressingly over her breasts, his touch seeming to scorch her through the thin cotton of her short nightie, but the heady excitement his gently teasing fingers aroused soon drowned all resistance. His mouth sought hers over and over again becoming more urgently demanding with each successive kiss and Anne felt desire leap and grow deep inside.

She felt a momentary chill when his arms, his mouth, released her and he leaned away from her. Dimly she was aware of his movement as he shrugged out of his robe and tossed it aside. The flame inside her leaped higher when he pulled her close against his nakedness. A fire with a need she didn't fully understand, inhibitions melting rapidly in that flame, she slid her hands along his body, loving the feel of his smooth warm skin. When she ran her fingers up and over his rigid, arched spine, he shivered and groaned against her mouth. "I could kiss you forever but, Anne, baby, it's no longer enough. Raise your arms."

She obeyed at once and sat meekly as he tugged her nightie up and over her head. When she was about to drop her arms, he caught her wrists in one of his hands and pulled them high over her head then forced her down against the bed. Stretched out below him, she felt her cheeks go pink as his eyes went slowly, burningly, over her body. Her color deepened when his hand followed the route his eyes had mapped out and her eyes closed with embarrassment when, without conscious thought, her body moved sensuously under his fingers.

"Open your eyes, Anne," he ordered softly, and when she did she found herself staring into warm liquid amber.

"Don't ever be embarrassed or ashamed with me. From tonight on, you are mine. You belong to me.

No, we belong to each other, for I am surely yours. There's no reason for you to be shy with me. You are beautiful and I love every inch of you. Do you understand?"

Unable to speak around the emotion blocking her throat, Anne nodded. He kissed her hard then whispered. "Tell me again that you love me, Anne."

"I love you, Jud, more than anything or anyone else on this earth."

Anne heard his breath catch and then his head lowered and his mouth followed the path of his eyes and hands, branding her with his ownership. They were both breathing heavily, almost painfully, when his hard body moved over hers and between short, fierce kisses, he vowed, "I love you, Anne. I'll always love you."

Neither one of them heard the door open and they both went rigid when Jud's father said coldly, "Get away from her, Jud."

Jud hesitated a second then through clenched teeth spat out, "Get the hell out of here, Dad."

"I told you to get away from her and I mean it. Now, move."

Judson Cammeron had not raised his voice, but there was an icy, angry command in his tone. Overwhelmed with disappointment and shame, Anne moaned softly, "Jud, please."

Jud remained still, every muscle in his body tense with anger, then he moved, slowly, pulling his robe over her body as he went.

Shaking with reaction, Anne lay listening to the silence crackle angrily between father and son. Her stepfather finally broke the silence. "Haven't you had enough with all the girls you've had in the last year? Must you bring your appetite home? Use your stepsister? Good God, man, she is little more than a child."

Jud started tightly, "Dad, you—" His father cut him off. "I'm taking Anne to her room, but I'll be back." He tucked the robe around her shaking body, then lifted her in his arms. At the door he paused, his voice thick with disgust. "Get some clothes on."

He carried her to her room, laid her on the bed, then turned his back to her, saying, "Put on a night-gown and get into bed. I'll be back, I'm going to get you something to help you sleep."

Tears running down her face, she leaped off the bed the minute he closed the door. With jerky move-ments she pulled a clean nightie over her head, crawled back into bed, turned her face into her pil-low, and sobbed brokenly.

By the time he returned she was shaking so badly he had to help her sit up and hold the glass for her while she chokingly swallowed the two pills he handed her.

"Don't cry so, Anne, you'll make yourself ill. I don't blame you in this, you're too young to under-stand."

"Mother?" Anne sobbed.

"She's asleep and I give you my word she, or any-one else, will not hear of this."

He left her and slowly, as the pills, whatever they were, took effect and she grew drowsy, the sobs sub-sided.

It had been late when Anne woke the next morn-ing. A beautiful Saturday morning that didn't fit at all with her depressed state. Feeling hurt, uncertain, very young, Anne showered and dressed, afraid to think about Jud and what had happened. She felt ashamed that her stepfather had found them the way they were, but she felt no guilt. She loved Jud and he said he loved her and their lovemaking, aborted though it had been, was a natural outpouring of that

28

love. Things might be uncomfortable for a while, but somehow she felt sure Jud would make it right. On that thought she had squared her shoulders and gone downstairs.

The twins were nowhere around, but her mother and stepfather were having mid-morning coffee in the living room. Anne started into the room, then stopped, a finger of fear stabbing her heart at their expressions. Her stepfather's face was set, stony. Her mother looked upset, near tears. Fearfully Anne asked, "What happened? Is something wrong?"

Judson opened his mouth, but before he could speak her mother cried. "Oh, Anne, it's Jud. Sometime during the night he packed his bags and left. He left no word of where he was going or when he'd be back, nothing."

Feeling her knees buckle, Anne dropped into a chair.

"But—"

The sight of her stepfather's eyes dried the words on her lips, for although his face was set, his eyes were filled with disappointment and despair. When he spoke, his voice was cold and flat.

"Margaret, I don't want his name mentioned in this house ever again, do you understand?"

"Judson!" her mother's voice mirrored her astonishment.

"I mean it," he went on in the same flat tone. "Talk to the twins, make them understand. Not ever again. Anne, do you understand?"

Anne had nodded her head bleakly, not understanding at all.

Anne, coming back to the present, stirred restlessly on the bed, eyes closed against the tears and pain that engulfed her. She had thought she had left the pain

29

behind a long time ago. At first she had waited hopefully for a phone call or a letter. But as the weeks became months the hope died, only the pain went on. As one year slipped into two, then three, the pain dulled, flaring at intervals as word of him began to reach them.

He had come into a sizable inheritance from his mother's estate the same day he left and he had used it well. Jud had always had a flair for the use of fabrics in clothes and he used that flair by opening an exclusive menswear shop. Somewhere he had run across two budding but avant garde designers and he hired them. They had obviously worked well together, for by the time Anne and his father heard of it, he had expanded to four stores in key cities. The first contact between Jud and his father had been made through Jud's assistant four years before.

Anne would never forget the look on Judson Cammeron's face the day he had called her into his office and silently handed her a letter. It had been a request for an interview to discuss the possibility of the production of a particular fabric and it had been signed by a John Franks, assistant to Judson Cammeron of Cammeron Clothiers. The only word that could describe her stepfather's expression was stunned.

Maintaining a rigid control she had asked quietly, "Will you see this John Franks?"

He had hesitated, then replied heavily, "We may as well, Anne. If we don't, they'll only go to the competition. Besides which, I'm curious to know what he has in mind for this fabric." He, of course, being Jud.

The meeting was held, a deal was struck, and they had been supplying Jud with special fabrics off and on ever since. But never at any time had personal contact been made between father and son. And at no time did Jud's name pass his father's lips although Anne knew by his attitude that he was pleased by even this small contact.

At last report Jud's stores numbered eight and he was reputed to be becoming a very rich man. The word that had filtered down to them was that there were some very wealthy men who bought almost exclusively from Jud and that their numbers were growing by the week.

And now, Anne thought, he would have it all. The company that produced the fabric, the designers who whipped up the original clothes, and the stores where they were sold. *Not all*, Anne corrected herself, *not if I can help it*. She had no right to any part of the company, but Troy and Todd did, and somehow she had to make sure they got it.

Suddenly Anne realized that her train of thought, the last few minutes, had alleviated, to a degree, her pain and shock. The tears were gone, replaced by determination. She had taken care of the twins since they were toddlers. Her protective, mother's instinct was to the fore replacing the hurt, humiliated feeling of that long-ago fifteen-year-old girl.

Her lips set in a determined line, Anne slid off the bed and walked to the window. The light was gone from the day that had never brightened above gray. Anne's room was on the side of the house and below, some distance beyond, the bright lights above the doors of the triple garage lit the surrounding area in an artificial glare. Eyes bleak as the weather, Anne studied the dark tracery of bare, black tree limbs. The stark branches in that eerie light had the effect of many arms raised in supplication to the heavens.

Restlessly she turned from the harsh etching, her eyes moving slowly over the muted pinks of the room bathed in the soft glow of the bedside lamp. She had

31

felt a measure of security in this room the last few years, had thought her shattered emotions healed, her heart becoming free once more. Now she felt scared, vulnerable, not unlike that tree outside with limbs lifted as if in yearning. She knew a longing deep inside that had to be quickly squashed.

Moving with purpose, she slowly undressed. She could show no sign of weakness with Jud, for if she did, she was sure he'd trample her as completely as would a wild, fear-crazed mob. She had allowed, no, invited, his trampling before. She wasn't sure she could survive it a second time.

Anne's head came up in defiance and her spine went taut with determination. She may have allowed him to hurt her, but she would not let him hurt her family. The thought that they were his family, too, was dismissed out of hand. He had disclaimed all rights to any of them ten years ago. The clock could not be turned back. All long-ago hurts—and words— were best forgotten. With a firm step she went into the bathroom.

CHAPTER

3

∽

I love you, Anne, I'll always love you. Singleminded determination was hard to hang onto with those words coming back to torment her. As she showered and dressed for dinner Anne berated herself for allowing the memory to creep back. There was no comparison between the Judson Cammeron who walked into the library today and the Jud who whispered those words so fervently all those years ago.

Misty-eyed, Anne stared at her reflection in the mirror, eyeshadow applicator poised over her right lid. She had managed to erase most of the evidence of her earlier weeping, and now, with the help of carefully applied makeup, was camouflaging the last traces.

She was definitely not looking forward to dinner. Would there be a replay of that earlier unpleasantness? Anne hoped not, but she had an uneasy feeling her hopes would be in vain. Jud seemed to be on a determined course of disruption with every one of them. Although, in all truth, he had been considerate of her mother's feelings, and his plan for Todd and Troy's future could, as he had said, be the making of them. But to her, his attitude bordered on vindictive. Why? Was it possible that those words of love rankled now? That hardly seemed possible. And anyway she, if anyone, had been the injured party in that farce.

Cloudy gray eyes studied their own reflection. What exactly did he have in mind? Anne puzzled at the question as she stroked smoky blue shadow over her eyelid. And why this insistence on his own secretary? Word of him in that department had filtered down to them too. If only half of the rumors they'd heard could be believed, Jud was a very busy boy indeed. She remembered the first time one such story had been circulated, and Jud's father's face when he'd relayed it to her. With something like pity she'd studied the warring emotions of pride and disgust he had revealed. It seemed, when it came to women, it was no-holds-barred with Jud. And, it appeared, the women were always exceptional. Beautiful, talented, rich.

Anne was an extremely fortunate young woman and she knew it. She was small and delicately formed. Her bone structure was good and covered by very soft, fine-textured skin. Her hair, a rich chocolate brown, was full and thick with a silky feel and healthy shine. Her eyes, normally a clear gray, changed color with her emotions. When she was happy or excited they grew lighter, almost silvery. But when she was angry, hurt, or felt something very deeply, they turned dark and stormy. Anne sighed as she brushed blusher onto her pale cheeks. She had been called lovely and, in all honesty, she supposed that was true, but she was not, in her own opinion, beautiful. Nor was she rich or very talented.

Her own thoughts brought her up short, and with a muttered "damn" she stood and moved away from the mirror. Whyever would she want to be any of those things? She did not have to be beautiful, rich, or talented. Just smart. Smart, and quick enough to protect her brothers' interests. She had no wish, she told herself, to attract Jud's interest, either physically or otherwise. Her Jud, the tender, loving Jud she'd secretly kept hidden inside her heart these last ten years, was just a figment of a young girl's romantic imagination. And the past was dead and buried. As dead and buried as the man who, unbeknownst to her, had saved her deep shame and humiliation when he'd walked into Jud's bedroom that night.

Squaring her shoulders resolutely, Anne left her room and walked quickly along the long hall and down the stairs. She was late. She could hear the others already in the dining room, and her mother's petulant voice ask, "Where is Anne?"

"Here." Anne spoke softly as she entered the room. "Sorry I'm late. You should have started."

The moment Anne was seated Mrs. Davis came through the door from the kitchen carrying a soup tureen and set it on the table, giving Anne a reproving look as she did so. Then, to Anne's astonishment, in a manner completely opposite of her earlier surliness, Mrs. Davis smiled ingratiatingly at Jud and murmured, "Would you like me to serve the soup now, Mr. Cammeron?"

"Yes. Thank you, Mrs. Davis." Jud's tone was quiet, pleasant, and authoritative all at the same time.

Anne felt a flash of irritation followed by a touch of fatalism. It certainly hadn't taken Mrs. Davis long to sniff out which way the wind was blowing.

During the early stage of the meal, conversation was minimal and stilted, and in the case of Troy and Todd, close to being rude. Anne herself had very little to offer and jumped with a startled "what?" when Jud rapped at her. "Who is the lucky man, and when is the big day?"

In confusion her eyes followed the direction of his and came to rest on the cluster of diamonds on her left hand. Andrew! Oh, Lord, she hadn't thought of him at all during this whole, horribly long day. Not since his call early in the morning. A deep flush mounting her cheeks, she lifted her eyes to Jud's face.

"Andrew Saunders, and we haven't set a date yet."

"Andrew Saunders." He repeated softly, then, his eyes mocking, his lower lip curled slightly. "Not the same Andy Saunders I chased home from school regularly?"

Anne felt her color deepen, but before she could form a suitably cutting retort, her mother chided, "That was a long time ago, Jud. Andrew is now a most respected, well-liked attorney. As a matter of fact he works for Mr. Slonne, and you know how particular he is."

Jud looked anything but chastised. One eyebrow rose mockingly and he turned to Anne with a bored drawl. "And where is the most respected and well-liked Andrew now?"

Anne moistened her lips, resentment burning through her at the ease with which he could put her on the defensive. Glancing up, she felt a funny catch of pain in her throat. Jud's eyes, a strange glow in their depths, were fastened intently on her mouth. A shock of pure, blind longing hit her like a blow and to negate the feeling she rushed into speech.

"H-he had to go out of town on business two days ago." Appalled at the breathless sound of her voice, Anne forced herself to slow down before adding, "Otherwise he would be here now. He will be back late tomorrow afternoon."

"I see."

Two words. Two very small words. And yet they seemed to speak volumes. His tone, that one brow arched so mockingly, seemed to say he saw far more than the simple fact that Andrew would return the following afternoon.

He can't possibly know, Anne told herself fiercely. No one can ever really know the depth of someone's feelings for another. Not really, can they? With a sigh of relief Anne heard her mother's soft voice change the conversation.

"Breakfast has always been ready at seven for your father and Anne, Jud. Will that be convenient for you also or would you prefer a different time?"

Finally Jud's disturbing gaze turned away from Anne's face to rest thoughtfully on his stepmother.

"I have already told you, Margaret, that I have no wish to disrupt the normal routine of this house," Jud answered quietly, then, on a snort from Todd, tagged on sardonically, "No more than absolutely necessary, that is."

He glanced up and smiled as Mrs. Davis entered the room to serve dessert and coffee. He waited until she was finished and was at the door to the kitchen again before he stated, "Breakfast at seven will be fine, Mrs. Davis. But don't plan on me for tomorrow morning, as I won't be here."

"Yes, sir."

The deference conveyed by Mrs. Davis's tone as she went through the door to the kitchen set Anne's teeth on edge. Yet her eyes swung, as did her mother's and the twins', to Jud, in question. Margaret voiced the question.

"But, Jud, where will you be?"

An expression of annoyance crossed Jud's face and, though it was fleeting, it left little doubt in any of their minds his irritation at having his movements questioned. Then, sighing softly, he answered. "I'm flying to New York in exactly"—he glanced at his

37

watch—"two hours. There are some things I want to collect from my office and my apartment." Glinting amber eyes flashed to Anne's face as he added, "Including my secretary. I'm booked on the early flight back tomorrow morning and I'll go right to the plant."

Anne barely heard his last sentence. Her mind was hung on his "including my secretary." His phrasing had made it sound as if his secretary was at his apartment. What was his secretary like, Anne wondered. Beautiful? Talented? Rich? A feeling of intense weariness swamped her, leaving her weak, slightly sick. *It's none of my business,* she told herself angrily forcing her attention back to the others as her mother asked, "Will you be home for dinner tomorrow night?" Margaret paused, then added nervously, "Andrew is coming to dinner and it would give you two a chance to get reacquainted."

"I wouldn't miss it for the world," Jud drawled, eyes again flashing mockingly at Anne. "Now, if you'll excuse me, I think I'd better make tracks or I'll miss my plane." He stood and strode to the door, then paused, turned back to the room, and asked, "Did you do as I asked, Anne?"

Anne felt the sense of weariness deepen, but lifting her head proudly she replied coolly. "Yes. Everything is in the briefcase on your father's desk."

His eyes grew sharp at her tone. Then, shrugging lightly, he murmured "Thank you" and left the room.

Quiet. Anne bit her lip, steeling herself for the storm that would surely follow this calm. Then it broke as the other three began speaking all at once. One hurt and two angry voices hurled questions at her. What were they going to do? What about their plans for Lauderdale? Did she think there was a chance of contesting the will? Who the hell did he think he was anyway? These questions and more along the same line, came from Todd and Troy. Wasn't it unfair to have to go to him for every penny? How could they possibly maintain a normal routine with his disruptive presence? Was there really anything any of them could do about it? Her mother had joined the questioners too.

Anne fielded the barrage as well as she could, knowing full well there was not a thing they could do. If there had been, she was sure that Mr. Slonne, being Mr. Slonne, would have indicated as much that afternoon.

Then it came. The question Anne had been dreading. What was she going to do?

"There really isn't too much I can do, is there?" Anne answered guardedly.

Three faces stared at her in astonishment long moments before Todd exclaimed, "What do you mean? Of course there is something you can do! All his big talk doesn't mean a thing if you stick with us. His hands will be tied, at least as far as the business is concerned."

"Todd is right, Anne." Her mother's voice held a mild tone of reproof. "Surely you don't intend to let him have his way?"

"I don't know exactly what I intend as yet." Anne sighed. "But I can't openly oppose him. He warned me that if I did he'd ruin the business. He assured me he could do this. I believe him; he wasn't bluffing."

"But that's stupid," Troy cried. "He'd stand to lose as much as we would. I think you're wrong. I believe he was bluffing."

Anne's head was moving from side to side in negation before Troy had finished speaking.

"Although you are right about Jud losing as much

as you, you forget he has another very successful operation to fall back on. You don't. Also, have you forgotten, he has control of the capital. He could cut you all down to the bare essentials. I'm not saying he would do that, just that he could, if his hand were forced. I'll leave it up to you. Do you want to take that chance? I do not appreciate the position your father has put me in, so I'll leave it up to you. If you want to make a fight of it I'll help you all I can, but I must be honest, and, in my opinion, we can't possibly win. Jud is smart and fast and, I'm afraid, more than a little ruthless. He won't quit until he has done exactly what he said he would."

"You want us to meekly obey every one of his damned orders?" Todd's face was a study of hurt disbelief, and Anne felt a shaft of irritation at the immaturity of both the question and the expression.

"What I want doesn't mean a damn thing," she snapped in exasperation. "I have merely pointed out the options open to you. What, exactly, do you expect me to do? I hold a very small amount of stock and I remain in this house on Jud's sufferance. So, you tell me, what do I do?"

Anne's voice had risen and she was visibly trembling. Breathing deeply, she brought herself under control and was about to add that she had already been ejected from the office but bit back the words. If they decided to make a fight of it, it wouldn't matter, and if they didn't, they'd know soon enough.

Glum silence had settled on the room at Anne's outburst and the expressions on all three of the faces in front of her were the same. They were stunned, shocked, and Anne knew they had expected some sort of miracle from her. Her inability to perform this miracle was a hard fact they did not want to face. But that she was as upset, if not more than they were, was evident, and after a long pause Todd said earnestly, "I'm sorry, Anne, I didn't think." He paused, wet his lips nervously, then went on. "I guess none of us thought this through. Too much has happened too fast. First the shock of Dad's death, then the sudden appearance of Jud, followed by the will and Jud's incredible dictums. I see now we have little choice, at least for the time being, but to follow Jud's lead. At least Troy and I can escape back to school; you have to face him every day."

"I just don't understand why Judson did this," Margaret sobbed, "after forbidding us to even mention Jud's name."

Anne considered then discarded the idea of telling her mother Jud's thoughts on why his father had acted as he had. What good would it do? she asked herself tiredly. It would just agitate them more and everyone was agitated enough already.

As they left the dining room, Troy slid his arm around Anne's waist. "This is one hell of a mess Dad's left us in," he murmured. Then he repeated Jud's statement of that afternoon. "And you're right in the middle, Anne."

Excusing herself, Anne went to her room and sat there staring moodily into space. It was a hell of a mess and she didn't want to be in the middle of it, didn't want to be exposed to Jud's obvious dislike and biting sarcasm.

Was there really anything she could do for Troy and Todd? Maybe if she could have remained in the office, but here? Anne shook her head. She doubted she'd see much of Jud at home. He didn't strike her as the type to spend his evenings in quiet companionship with his family. Especially this family.

Then a new idea struck her. Maybe Andrew could advise her. True he knew little of the business, as Mr.

Slonne and his partners had handled all of the company's legal work. But as a member of the firm, even a fairly junior member, he'd handled some of the minor work. And Andrew was an intelligent young man. Although reluctant to involve him in her family's infighting, Anne clutched at Andrew's name as at a lifeline. At the moment, she felt utterly helpless and Andrew was a ray of hope. It didn't occur to her that Andrew, being her fiancé, should have been the first person to turn to.

Anne had a restless night, dozing and waking repeatedly, and when she did finally fall into an exhausted sleep close to dawn, it was tormented by a nightmare.

They were swimming in a place Anne didn't recognize, and Troy and Todd were out much too far. About to call to them to come back, Anne saw them begin to flounder, then cry out for help. She struck out boldly to go to them, when she was brought up short by strong, hard fingers grasping her ankle. Two hands of steel, moving hand over hand up her leg, towed her back. "Let me go," she screamed wildly. "They'll die out there."

"You know the rules of the game." The voice was cold, menacing. Jud's voice. "It's sink or swim, live or die, winner take all."

Frantically she fought the coils of steel on her body, sputtering and choking on the churning water that splashed into her mouth. Her struggle was meaningless, for the hard hands grasped her shoulders, hauled her around to face him. In sheer terror she cried out at his look. Tall enough to stand where she could not, he seemed to tower over her, and the expression on his face was threatening, almost diabolical. Fear and panic increased her struggles and she fought desperately to free herself.

"If you insist on fighting me," he intoned icily, "there is only one thing I can do." With that he shoved her back, away from him, and, although she knew the impetus of the motion would completely submerge her, she felt a wild surge of hope as she felt his fingers loosen their painful hold. The hope was quickly dashed as she felt his arms slide around her back. He was going to follow her under—no, he was forcing her under, his large frame on top of her forcing her down, down. As the water covered her chin, she drew a great breath of air, then felt shock grip her mind, for Jud's mouth covered hers, forcing her lips apart, at the same instant the water covered her head, cutting off the life-sustaining air.

What was he doing? Was he trying to drown them both? But no, Jud was an expert swimmer; he had always amazed everyone with the length of time he could remain under water. Terror crawled through her veins like a slithering reptile. He was going to kill her! A scream grew in her chest and lodged in her throat, unable to escape, and her mind throbbed with the words "I don't want to die! I don't want to die!" Panic increased her struggles and the sinewy arms tightened, crushing her against his hard, slippery body as his legs encircled hers in a pincer embrace. Then the pressure against her mouth subtly changed, became caressing, sensuous and suddenly the fear coursing through her body changed too, became a searing tongue of desire, licking and consuming all other emotion. Their frenetic spiral under water became an erotic ballet, with his possession, and her death, the finale. And she didn't care. More, she welcomed it, somehow knowing his possession would be worth it. Roughly the panties to her bikini were torn from her, and, joy singing through her, she arched her body to his.

At that moment Anne surfaced from the nightmare, her body bathed in a cold sweat. Her hands were clutching the bedcovers and she was shaking and sobbing low in her throat. Breathing deeply, Anne finally brought her shattered emotions under control, except for the occasional shudder. The dream had been so real, was still so vivid and clear in her mind.

Afraid to go back to sleep again, she lay back against the pillow and stared at the window, watching the pale gray first light turn to shell pink day.

Anne's cheeks flushed the same shell pink as flashes of the dream skipped in and out of her mind. There were some parts of it she thought she understood. Troy and Todd's drowning, her effort to save them, Jud's keeping her from doing so. If she could find no way of helping them, Troy and Todd would go under—financially. And Jud had made it quite clear he intended to keep her from helping them.

But the rest of the dream? Anne felt a tremor slide down her spine. Did she believe, subconsciously, that Jud would go as far as physically harming her to get what he wanted? Her mind firmly skirted around the sexual connotations, putting that part down to her memories of ten years before. Nevertheless she felt a warmth invade her body, a longing ache tug at her throat. Was it possible to want someone so badly you would even welcome oblivion to taste that sweetness just once?

Anne shook her head firmly. *Nonsense, forget it, it was only a dream, all of it.* Yet, at the back of her mind she felt a small, but very real, twinge of fear.

As dawn blossomed into full morning, anxiety grew inside Anne. If she'd been able to keep to her usual routine, she assured herself, she could have controlled

44

it, but with time on her hands, her mind ran rampant with speculation.

She was pacing her room when her mother called her to the phone. Glad for any excuse to escape her own confused thoughts, Anne raced down the steps and across the foyer to the telephone table. Breathless from her run, she almost gasped, "Hello?"

"Where the hell are you?" Jud's voice was a hard rap against her ears.

"Obviously I'm here at home," Anne snapped, all her fears of the last hours lacing her tone with ice. "What do you want?"

"What do I want?" he repeated angrily. "I want you, that's want the hell I want. You have exactly thirty minutes to get that pretty little tush of yours down here. If you're not here by then I'll come after you, so snap it."

CHAPTER

4

Anne winced at the loud noise that assaulted her ear as Jud slammed down his receiver. Confusion and shock kept her immobile a few moments then the words "snap it" echoed through her mind and, spinning on her heel, she ran up the stairs. His tone had left little doubt that he'd do exactly as he threatened.

Thirty-two minutes later she walked into the office she still thought of as hers and came face to face with a tall, willowy, gorgeous redhead.

"May I help you?"

The cool, well-modulated voice perfectly matched the appearence of the redhead and Anne felt a disquieting, sinking sensation. So this was the secretary Jud had to have in his office. She was certainly beautiful and more than likely very talented, and with the first two attributes, rich hardly seemed important.

Breathing deeply, Anne managed to answer quietly. "Yes, I'm Anne Moore. Mr. Cammeron is expec—"

At that moment one of the two doors behind the redhead opened and Jud snapped impatiently, "It's about time. Come in here, Anne." He held the door to what had been his father's office open, his amber gaze steady on her face as Anne walked past him into the large room.

It seemed like weeks rather than days since Anne had been in this office and she glanced around warily somehow expecting changes. Of course there were none, except for the fact that the top of Judson Senior's large oak desk, usually so neat and orderly, was a welter of folders and loose papers. The room was exactly the same.

Anne's eyes noted the desk top as they quickly scanned the brown and white tweed carpet, the tan burlap-weave draperies, the crammed bookshelf along one wall, and the three leather-covered chairs in front of the desk. At the same time her mind registered the warmer shading of Jud's tone as he spoke to his secretary.

"I'll be busy for the rest of the day, Lorna. I'll accept no calls except from the list of names I gave you earlier. Take your lunch at the usual time. And would you bring back a couple of sandwiches for Miss Moore and me?"

"Yes, sir."

The secretary's reply was punctuated by the soft click of the door being closed. Anne turned, a small lump catching at her throat as she viewed Jud. He leaned almost indolently against the door, his gold hair and bronze skin set off by the deep brown of his suit and the crisp white of his shirt.

"All right, Anne." His voice was soft and silky. Too silky. "What's the play?"

"I don't know what you mean." Anne had trouble covering the tremor in her voice.

His mouth took on the by now familiar sardonic twist. His eyes mocked her. "Were you going to show as much disrespect of me as possible by coming in very late or weren't you going to come in at all?"

Anne stared at him in disbelief a moment then rushed her words angrily. "You said you didn't need me in this office!"

"No, I did not," he stated flatly before jerking his thumb over his shoulder at the door. "I said I didn't need you in that office."

Since entering the room, Anne had been aware of scraping, shuffling noises from the adjoining, smaller office, the office Jud had occupied over ten years ago. His next words explained the muffled sounds.

"I'm having my old office cleaned up for you. I take it it has been used for storage for some time now?"

Anne nodded dumbly.

"Yes, well," he grimaced, "until it can be made ready for you, you'll have to work in here with me."

"Doing what exactly?"

"For heaven's sake, Anne, what do you think?" Jud sighed and pushed himself away from the door and moved across the room toward her. "I'm no more a fool than the old man was. For the next few weeks your help in here will be invaluable to me. That's why I brought Lorna back with me. To free you of the outer office work."

Her voice strained, Anne asked, "And after the next few weeks?"

Jud paused, his eyes raking her tight, closed face. "I'll probably dump even more work on you. I have two separate companies to run, Anne. And I have no intention of giving up the reins to either one of them. If the going gets tough you can cry on John Franks's shoulder. As I'm sure you already know, John is my other assistant."

His assistant! A small shiver of pleasure shot through Anne. Not only was he not banishing her from the office, he wanted her for his assistant. Anne

48

felt tears of relief sting her eyes and blinked quickly, then her eyes flew wide as he stepped in front of her and grasped her shoulders tightly.

"I expect you to give me the same loyalty and everything else you gave the old man." His voice had taken on a thick roughness. A small shiver slid down Anne's spine. "Beginning with this." His head dipped swiftly, then his mouth was crushing hers in a brutal, painful kiss.

Anne went rigid with shock, unable, for a moment, to think or move. Then her mouth was released and he moved back, away from her.

"What do you think you're doing?" Wildly confused and angry, Anne nearly choked on the words.

"I just told you," Jud answered in a bored tone, turning his back to her as he walked around the desk. "I expect all the fringe benefits the old man had." He turned back to her sharply, his voice nasty. "Were you naive enough to think that your—how should I say it—devotion to my father had gone unnoticed? Or that the word hadn't spread?"

As his words hammered at her, Anne's mind filled with horror. What was he saying? Surely no one in their right mind would think that she and her stepfather were . . . Unable to bear the thought, Anne cried, "What do you mean? Exactly what are you accusing me of?"

"Come off it, Anne, it's been whispered about for some time now." Jud's face and voice were cold, his mouth an unremitting, hard line. "It's nothing very new or novel. An older man seeking the virility of his youth with a young woman. Or, in this case, you endeavoring to show your gratitude in whatever way he wished. Or did you convince yourself you were in love with him?"

Struck speechless, anger gripping her throat, Anne

stared at him for several long minutes. Then the anger exploded from her mouth. "Are you out of your dirty little mind? He was my mother's husband."

"Are you telling me there was nothing of a personal nature between you?" Jud's tone was skeptical, his eyes sharp.

"I am telling you exactly that." Anne drew a deep breath in an effort to control the tremor of anger in her voice. "Not only do you insult me, you smear your father's memory. Have you grown so cynical, so jaded over the years that you'd believe something like that about a man like your father? I don't know what happened between you to cause the break in your relationship, and it's none of my business. But I'll tell you this. At no time was your father other than kind and considerate toward me. He treated me like a daughter, and yes, I was loyal and I was grateful. He was a good man, the closest thing to a father I ever knew. Now, if you are quite through trying to humiliate me with your filthy suggestions, I'll leave. I have a lot of packing to do."

Anne's fingers loosened from the back of the chair she was gripping and she turned and took two steps toward the door, only to stop at Jud's ordered "Stay where you are."

She was almost relieved to obey his command, for her legs were shaking so badly she wasn't sure she could take another step. Atlhough his hands were gentle, she flinched when he touched her arms, turned her to face him.

"I'm sorry, Anne." His amber eyes were shadowed, cloudy with some emotion Anne couldn't define. His voice was soft and contrite. "I had no right to say what I did. I should have challenged the innuendo when I first heard it. I was bitter and, in that bitterness, believed it. Time and distance and circumstances can have a big effect on a man's thinking. I was out of line and I apologize. Don't leave, either this office or the house. Your mother, Troy, and Todd need you at the house. And whether you believe it or not, I need you here."

Anne lowered her eyes, fighting the tears that had been building for the last ten minutes. Her instinct for self-preservation urged her to run, but she wanted so badly to stay. Breathing slowly, she regained control and lifting her head proudly she said, "All right, Jud, I'll stay. At least temporarily. I owe that to Todd and Troy. But I warn you, if ever I hear you mention anything about your father and—"

"You won't." Jud cut in firmly. "Not from me or anyone else. You have my word on that."

The atmosphere was heavy with tension as Jud turned from her to pick up a chair and place it next to his own behind the desk. Anne stood motionless watching him until, lifting his head, one eyebrow raised, he said softly, "There really is a lot of work here, Anne. And I really could use your help."

Anne sighed as she slipped out of her coat and hung it up before moving around the desk to sit down beside him. He could still be persuasive if he wanted to, she thought ruefully, that was one area in which he hadn't changed.

"What I want to do first is go over the personnel files of everyone in any kind of a managerial position down to the last foreman and forelady and quality control person."

Pulling a folder from the pile he opened it on the desk between them and began firing questions at her.

The tension in the room soon dissipated as Anne, at times, found herself reaching for answers to Jud's sharply incisive queries. She became fully absorbed in the work and didn't notice the passage of time until a soft tap on the door and Jud's growled "Come in" brought her head up.

"Your lunch, Mr. Cammeron."

Anne watched as Jud's secretary walked gracefully across the room. Before she was halfway to the desk, Jud was out of his chair and relieving her of the tray she was carrying.

"Thank you, Lorna. I'll settle up with you later."

"Yes, sir." The door closed quietly on the softly spoken words.

As he slid the tray onto the edge of the cluttered desk, Jud said crisply. "Come on, Anne, take a break and have something to eat."

Suddenly hungry, Anne's eyes went to the tray of food. On it were two Styrofoam cups of soup, a paper plate piled with sandwiches, a pot of coffee, a small sugar bowl and creamer, two mugs, and two paper napkins. She reached for a cup of soup at the same time Jud did, and when his fingers brushed hers she jerked her hand away as if burned.

Cold amber eyes mocking her nervousness, lips twisting in a sardonic smile, Jud picked up both cups of soup, and handing one to her, carefully drawled, "I don't bite, Anne. At least, not very often."

Pink-cheeked, Anne lowered her eyes only to lift them again as she heard him sigh in exasperation and turn away to walk to the window behind the desk. Sipping the creamed tomato soup, Anne studied him through the fringe of her lashes. The bright afternoon sunlight slanting through the window struck sparks of glinting gold off his hair, brought a glistening sheen to his bronze skin. Anne shivered as the words tawny gold crept into her mind. Even as a teen-ager Jud had been handsome. Now, with maturity and experience etched onto his face, he was devastating.

Wanting to look away but unable to unfasten her eyes from his broad back, a second shiver followed the first when Jud arched his spine and flexed his shoulders. During the morning, while they had been deep into the work, he had shrugged out of his jacket, loosened his tie, and opened the top button of his shirt. Now, the play of muscles under the fine material of his shirt as he stretched, one hand going to massage the back of his neck, sent a shaft of feeling through Anne so intense it robbed her of her breath.

Jerking her eyes away, she forced herself to finish her soup and reach for a piece of sandwich she didn't want.

"Why don't you get up and walk around awhile, Anne?"

Concentrating on eating the unwanted food, Anne hadn't heard Jud move away from the window and his voice, so close beside her, made her jump. Impatience laced his tone as he snapped, "For God's sake, will you relax? From the look on your face, anyone walking in right now would think I had hit you."

Anne glanced up as he moved around the desk, his face and body taut with anger. He filled the mugs with coffee, picked up the cream, and raised his brows in question, his hands pausing over the mugs. She nodded as she stood up. "I'm sorry. You startled me, I thought you were still at the window." He handed her one of the mugs without speaking, his eyes, hard and cold, searching her face. Unable to withstand his intent gaze, Anne took the mug with a murmured "thank you" and turned away to retrace his steps to the window.

Anne gulped her coffee, tears stinging her eyes when the hot liquid scorched her mouth. *What have*

I let myself in for? she thought frantically. How can I work with him if every move he makes, every word he utters unnerves me like this?

Jud moved to stand behind her, making deliberate noises as he walked across the room. Even so, when his fingers lightly touched her arm she could not repress a small shiver. He sighed softly, then said quietly, "Anne, look at me."

Anne stiffened, then forcing her unseeing eyes from the parking lot in front of the large factory building, she turned to face him.

"We're never going to be able to work together if you tighten up like this every time I come near you, Anne." Jud's tone was still soft, but a definite firmness underlined his words. "I realize this isn't easy for you, especially after my behavior earlier. But if you intend to stick to your word and stay, you are going to have to push your dislike of me to the back of your mind at least here in the office."

"Jud—"Anne began, but he raised his hand and interrupted, all softness gone now.

"Let me finish. I'm going to be under a lot of pressure during the next few months. Besides the work here I have a number of things on the fire in connection with my clothing business. I'm probably not going to be the easiest man in the world to get along with and I can't have you around if you're going to be this uptight all the time. I've admitted I need your help here, so I'll leave it up to you. If you can't handle it, tell me. If you're going to stay, you'll have to bury your resentment." He paused, his cool eyes raking her face. Then he snapped, "What is it going to be, Anne, go or stay?"

"I told you before I'd stay, Jud. I haven't changed my mind," Anne answered steadily.

"Good." His right hand was held out as he added. "Peace?"

Anne hesitated, then placed her hand in his, felt a tiny shock run up her arm as his hard fingers clasped hers, but managed a calm, "All right, Jud, peace."

The afternoon flew by even faster than the morning had and when Jud's phone buzzed around four thirty Anne was grateful for the opportunity to stretch while Jud answered it. She heard him say, "Who is it, Lorna?" then, "Okay, put it through." Then he held the receiver out to Anne. She gave him a surprised glance, but he didn't say anything, just smiled—mockingly, she thought.

"Hello?" She spoke uncertainly.

"Anne? Is that you, darling?" Andrew's voice came warm over the wire.

"Yes, Andrew. When did you get home?" Somehow Anne infused some warmth of her own into her tone, wondering why it should be so difficult.

"Just now, who answered your phone?"

"Jud's secretary." Anne said without thinking.

"Jud?" Andrew's voice had sharpened. "Jud Cammeron? When did he get back and what's he doing in your office?"

Anne sighed. Of course Andrew wouldn't know about the will and, by the way Jud's face was tightening in anger at the interruption, she couldn't tell Andrew now. Hurriedly she said, "He's not in my office, I'm in his," and looked up to see one white brow arch arrogantly. "I can't talk now, as we're very busy. I'll explain tonight. You are coming for dinner?"

"Yes, but—" he began, but Anne cut him off. "I have to go now, Andrew, see you at the house. Goodbye." Before he could reply, she hung up, sat down at the desk, and picked up the folder she and Jud had been working on.

"So the legal eagle is back." Jud chided smoothly, the very smoothness of his tone irritating. "How nice for you. Now, do you think we could finish this folder before you have to rush home to get ready for him?"

"Jud, really—" Anne began warningly.

"Anne, really," Jud cut in sarcastically, then his tone softened. "Okay, I'm sorry for the dig. Tell you what. I promise to be on my best behavior tonight at dinner, if you will."

"What do you mean, if I will?"

"Just what I said. I'll be polite and charming to Andrew, if you'll reciprocate with Lorna."

"Lorna?" Anne repeated, stunned. "Lorna is coming to dinner tonight?"

"Yes."

"But—"

"But nothing," Jud said icily. "I called Margaret this morning and told her. She understood, even if you don't."

Oh, I understand perfectly, Anne thought scathingly, trying to ignore the sudden twist of pain that shot through her chest. What's to understand? A man brings his mistress to town, what else does he do but invite her home to dinner! *Oh, God, I feel sick.* Why? Before she had to face an answer to that why, she rushed into speech.

"Of course I'll be polite to her. Why shouldn't I be?" She hesitated, then added, "She's a very beautiful woman."

"Yes, she is." Hard finality in his tone, cold and flat as his eyes. Unable to maintain that intent stare, Anne turned back to the work on the desk, shocked at the way her fingers were trembling.

* * *

Sinking into the scented bath water, Anne sighed wearily. She was tired. It had been a long, emotionally charged day, with Jud not letting up until almost six o'clock. Now, little less than an hour later, Anne wished for nothing more than to lie back in the tub and forget the evening ahead. She couldn't, of course. In fact, she should be downstairs at this moment as Andrew would be arriving any minute.

Sighing again, Anne finished her bath, stepped out of the tub, gave herself a quick, vigorous rub with a large bath towel, and swung around to lift her robe from the hook on the bathroom door. A flashing reflection made her pause, then stop completely to contemplate the nude young woman gazing back at her from the full-length mirror on the door.

Beginning at the top of her head, Anne's eyes critically evaluated the image before her. Her hair, dark and sleek, was cut close to her head on the top and sides, a natural wave giving it a sculptured look. The back was a little longer, turning in softly to caress her neck. The face, to Anne's eyes, though pleasing, held a sad, somewhat wistful look, too thin, too pale, and the eyes seemed enormous, with a vaguely lost expression. Her small frame was slender, too slender. Although Anne admitted it was well formed—the small breasts high and rounded, the waist tiny, the hip and legline smooth and supple.

Anne's sigh this time was deeper, almost painful. Her head and shoulders sagged and she closed her eyes to shut out the vision before her. The girl in the mirror was pleasing, yes, but hardly competition for the tall, willowy, exquisitely beautiful redhead who would be joining them for dinner.

The thought jerked her upright and eyes wide and incredulous stared back at her. Competition? Why had she thought that? She was in no way in any kind of competition with Lorna or any other woman in connection with Jud. Jud was everything she disliked in a man. Arrogant, ruthless, probably even conceited. Also, probably not above using his blatant good looks to get what he wanted.

A picture of him formed in her mind. She could see him as he'd been at times that afternoon when her answers had not quite satisfied him. He had pushed back his chair impatiently and prowled—prowled, exactly like the lions she had gone to see at the zoo in Philadelphia as a little girl—back and forth, as if trying to wear out the carpet. She had felt breathless and strangely excited by his powerful, masculine, overtly sexy look. Even now, hours later, the memory brought a shallowness to her breathing, a tight ache to the pit of her stomach.

In self-disgust Anne pulled open the bathroom door and hurried along the hall to her bedroom. Quickly, but carefully, she dressed and applied a light makeup, all the while telling herself that Jud Cammeron meant nothing to her. He was a force to be reckoned with, but that was all.

Really? Chided a small, amused voice at the very edge of her consciousness. *Then why does the mere thought of going down those stairs and entering the living room set your heart thumping into your throat?* Swallowing painfully, Anne hesitated, her hand pausing in the act of opening her door. *Because,* she told that tiny voice, *because I'm afraid of him. He is a dangerous adversary who holds my brothers' futures in the palms of his strong, capable hands. Without warning, he could close those hands into a tight fist and crush all their hopes and plans.*

And possibly your spirit as well? The small unrepentent voice asked slyly.

As if fleeing a demon, Anne tore out of the room

and down the stairs, forcing herself to slow down as she reached the entrance to the living room.

Andrew was there, and yet the first person her eyes went to was Jud. Good Lord, he was devastating in close-fitting brown slacks and a tan silk shirt. The clothes, combined with his hair and skin coloring, lent an allover tawny appearance. *A tawny gold man,* Anne thought crazily, fighting to control the jumbled sensations eating away at her poise.

"There you are, darling." Andrew's voice, as he came across the room to her, helped restore some of her equilibrium. "I was beginning to think you must have fallen asleep." His tone was light, teasing and as he bent to kiss her he added softly, "I've missed you. Was it very bad? And what's the story with Jud? Your mother seems almost afraid of him."

Anne managed a strained smile and whispered, "I'll explain later, when we're alone. I missed you too."

Thankful for the support of Andrew's hand at her waist, Anne moved into the room, a shaft of dismay sliding through her as her eyes encountered Jud's secretary. The red hair that had been drawn back neatly into a twist at the back of her head during the day had been set free to become a loose, glowing flame around her beautiful face. The tall, sleek body was encased in a hot-pink sheath that gave proof to all of her perfect figure.

With the urge to turn and run crawling up her spine, Anne was amazed at the cool composure of her voice as she acknowledged Jud's formal introduction.

"In my haste to get started this morning I'm afraid I forgot to introduce you two." Jud lied smoothly. Then his voice seemed, to Anne's ears, to change to a warm caress as he drew Lorna toward her. "Lorna,

I'd like you to meet my"—he paused—"stepsister, Anne Moore. Anne, my secretary, Lorna Havers."

Cool fingers touched Anne's equally cool ones as Lorna murmured throatily, "I'm pleased to meet you, at last, Miss Moore."

Anne barely had time to reply, "Call me Anne, please, Lorna," when Jud informed, "I have already introduced Lorna to Andrew and your mother, Anne." His voice went hard before he added, "The twins haven't put in an appearance as yet."

He couldn't have said anything more calculated to inject steel into her spine if he had tried. Anne opened her mouth to fly to her brothers' defense, when they strolled into the room, completely unaware of the tension within. As a single unit they stopped dead in their tracks, eyes widening as they caught sight of Lorna.

A small smile of amusement tugging at her mouth, Anne turned to Andrew, and the smile and amusement vanished. Andrew's eyes reflected the admiration evident in Troy's and Todd's, and along with it was an expression Anne could only interpret as calculating speculation. Turning away quickly, Anne felt a small flicker of alarm, for Jud stood watching the tableau, a cool, mocking gleam in his amber eyes, the familar sardonic twist on his mouth. And what caused Anne's alarm was the fact that Jud was observing Andrew closely.

With relief Anne heard Mrs. Davis announce dinner. Her relief was short-lived for after they were all seated, all the conversation except for the occasional remark tossed to her mother and herself centered on Lorna. And through it all Jud sat, the same amused expression on his face, watching—watching.

Watching for what? Anne asked herself irritably, pushing the food around on her plate. Watching for those three fools to make complete asses of themselves over his secretary-mistress? Unable to decipher the expression Jud wore, Anne had to admit she didn't know what he was watching for, and she hastened to assure herself that she didn't really care.

What an unbelievably long night, Anne thought tiredly some four hours later, as she slid between her sheets. Long and not too good for her ego. As dinner had begun, so had the evening progressed—all the men's attention on Lorna. Her mother had retreated shortly after dinner, leaving Anne to her own devices, of which she had few. And to top it off she had not had that private talk with Andrew. She had so longed for the chance to tell him all that had happened, ask his advice. Now she was almost glad the chance had not come her way. The wish to confide in him had curiously vanished.

All evening—as Jud had watched all of them—Anne had observed Andrew in growing disbelief. Quiet, calm, clearheaded Andrew was as bowled over by Lorna as the immature, lighthearted Troy and Todd. What had happened to the almost pompous seriousness of the man she was engaged to?

A few years younger than Jud, Anne had known Andrew most of her life. Their mothers had been friends for years, although he hadn't seemed aware of Anne at all until a few years ago.

Twisting Andrew's ring around her finger, Anne compared the smiling, eager, handsome man who had danced attendance on Lorna all evening with the coolly reserved, sharp-minded Andrew she had become engaged to. She had never heard him laugh so much, had never seen him so animated. Strangely the most surprising thing he'd done all evening was rake his fingers through his hair, ruffling its usual dark smoothness. Anne had never seen him with a hair out of place. Even she would not have dared to bring disorder to that neatness, and oddly, she had never had the urge to do so.

She had always felt safe and secure with Andrew. Now that security was shaken. Disturbed and confused by the events of the last few days, Anne felt alone and vulnerable, and more than a little afraid.

CHAPTER

5

Jud kept Anne so busy during the following weeks, she barely noticed the last dying gasp of winter or the slow, inexorable advance of spring. He set a grueling pace for himself and, in determination, she strove to keep up with him. She fell into bed exhausted every night and grew even more slender and yet she had never felt more alive in her life. Jud seem to charge everything and everyone around him with electricity, and his energy seemed endless. Unfortunately his temper had a much shorter span and Anne had felt or witnessed the sharp edge of his tongue too often for comfort. No one, from top management to the night watchman, escaped his notice, be it to administer a rebuke or to praise. What amazed Anne was that, by April, when Todd and Troy came home for the spring break, the majority of the employees looked on Jud as a kind of god.

Anne herself had mixed feelings about him. Honesty made her admit he had a brilliant business mind. He missed nothing, however small and seemingly unimportant, and had succeeded, more than once, in making Anne feel incompetent. Grudgingly she admitted to herself he did not do it on purpose. She ached with the need to find fault with his handling of the company, and with growing frustration realized that need would not be assuaged.

She had moved into her own office at the end of the first week, then wondered why Jud had even bothered to have it made ready for her, as the connecting door between the two rooms was always left open and his barked "Anne come in here" had her running back and forth as if she were a yo-yo at the end of a string he had tied around his finger.

By the end of her second week, to her surprise, Lorna returned to his New York office, having trained a replacement in a few days' time. Jud's new secretary—a Mrs. Donna Kramer—was a highly qualified, thirty-eight-year-old widow, with three teen-age sons. An attractive, friendly woman, Anne liked her at first meeting and despite their age difference a warm friendship was developing. More surprising still was the fact that Jud hardly seemed to notice Lorna's absence, even though he had been out of the office until after lunch on the day her plane left.

To Anne Jud was an enigma, never quite behaving as she would expect. She had not expected him to spend much time at home, so, of course, he was there most evenings. Even though he did close himself in the library, he was home. She had expected him to treat her mother with cool reserve, so, contrarily, he was all warm consideration toward her. The reserve he saved for Anne, who had expected mockery and sarcasm.

And as if she didn't have enough on her mind keeping up with Jud, Andrew baffled Anne. He seemed to be changing somehow, and Anne found herself wondering if she really knew him as well as she had thought she did.

On the Saturday night after Jud's return, he took her out for dinner and his choice of restaurant was in

64

itself unusual. The inn, on the outskirts of Philadelphia, though expensive, was quiet and secluded. As a rule he chose a restaurant closer to home and always a place where he could see, and would be seen by, his friends and colleagues. From the beginning of their relationship Anne had been aware of the fact that Andrew was very ambitious. He intended to move up in the legal profession, not only in their own small community some fifteen miles outside of Philadelphia, but in Philadelphia itself. He had never confided to Anne how he planned to do this, but that his plans were rigidly laid out in his own mind had always been evident.

Anne had accepted Andrew's first invitation to go out with him the previous spring, less then a year ago. She had accepted his proposal and ring three months ago. Yet, in all that time, he had never found it necessary to share a quiet intimate dinner with her. When he ushered her into the subdued, underplayed elegance of the old inn, the questions, and a vague uneasiness, began to stir in Anne.

Their dinner was expertly prepared and delicious and as they sipped their after-dinner coffee and liqueur, Anne studied Andrew through the shield of her lashes. His height was the only thing average about him. His smoothly brushed dark hair looked almost too perfect to be real, as did the matinee idol handsomeness of the face beneath it. His body was slender and compact, kept in peak condition by vigorous workouts at the local racquet club. His manners were impeccable and his attitude toward her had always been one of polite consideration. In essence Andrew was a cool, analytical mind in a well-dressed, attractive body.

Their relationship, so far, had been comfortable and emotionless, a fact that had gone a long way in her decision to accept his proposal. His casual love-making had always been just that—casual and un-demanding. Anne felt safe with him because, for reasons she did not care to examine too closely, she herself shied away from any deep emotional involvement. But tonight there was a subtle difference in Andrew, a difference that made Anne uncomfortable.

"Where are you, darling?"

Andrew's quiet voice nudged Anne out of her reverie. Her eyes refocused on his somber face and she laughed shakily.

"I'm sorry, Andrew."

"What were you thinking about?" He probed. "Are you having problems in the office?"

Anne knew by the tone of his voice that he was feeling excluded. Andrew was still not fully in the picture as to her stepfather's will and its aftereffects. She had been so busy all week, thanks to Jud, not only during the day, but in the evenings as well. He had asked, no ordered, if politely, her into the library the last two nights to explain some business papers he'd found in his father's desk. Therefore the opportunity to talk to Andrew had not materialized.

Now, seeing Andrew's face grow grim and stubborn, Anne plunged into an explanation.

"You mean you are all literally under his thumb?" he asked in astonishment when she'd finished.

"To a degree, yes," Anne answered softly. "Needless to say Troy and Todd resent him and his dictates like hell. But there is very little any one of us can do about it. He's a veritable slave driver in the office, and yet no one there seems to resent him too much. Possibly because he drives himself harder than anyone else."

"But this is untenable for you, Anne. You cannot

possibly go on working day and night for this man simply because his father saw fit to insult you with ten percent of the stock. I find it hard to believe that he, or the twins for that matter, has not offered to buy the stock from you."

He, this man—Anne had not missed Andrew's refusal to use Jud's name. Sighing softly, she said wearily, "As a matter of fact they have offered to buy the stock. All of them. I do not want to sell it."

His eyes narrowed, but before he could voice his objection, Anne held out her hand placatingly, pleading, "Andrew, let me explain, please."

He looked on the verge of refusing, then nodded angrily.

"All right, but I'm damned if I can see a reasonable explanation for you putting up with his arrogance."

"In the first place," Anne admonished, "I do not feel insulted by Judson's bequest. True, as practically everyone has been eager to point out, he virtually left me in the middle, between his sons. But equally true, as Jud was only too happy to point out, Judson was fairly certain I would not sell or give my share to any of them."

"But why, for heaven's sake?" Andrew's growing impatience was beginning to show in the tone of his voice, the brightness of his usually cool, brown eyes.

"Simply because, in all conscience, I can't. Oh, Andrew, surely you of all people understand. If I sell, or give, the stock to Troy and Todd, they'll force Jud out and in their inexperience ruin the company. And if I sell"—no hint at the word *give* here—"to Jud, he'll take over completely. At least this way he is under some control."

"Precious damn little, I'd say, with a man like him," Andrew snapped. Then his legal mind reassert-

67

ed itself, and he added, "But I do see your position. Not an enviable one either. But, Anne darling, how long is this tug-of-war likely to go on?"

"I don't know," Anne answered tiredly. "Right now the twins are in silent rebellion, but I'm hoping they pull themselves together and get down to the business of learning the business. The moment I feel they can handle the company, and Jud, I'll gladly hand over the stock. I don't really want it, as I feel I have no right to it in the first place."

"What! But that's ridiculous," Andrew exclaimed. "You were like a daughter to Mr. Cammeron. I would have thought he'd leave you much more. And when the time comes there will be no talk of giving anything to anyone. You have as much right to your legacy as he has, if not more. He's the deserter, not you."

Anne glanced up sharply, the unease she'd felt earlier doubling in proportion. What had gotten into Andrew? Never before had he assumed that proprietorial attitude toward her. But even more disquieting was the nasty edge to his tone whenever he spoke of Jud. As if he actually hated while at the same time envied him. But why? Anne had no answer to that, and so felt totally lost and confused. Besides which, she was just too tired to go into it with him. Reaching across the table, she touched his hand lightly.

"Andrew, please, I'm really very tired. Could we leave this discussion for another time?"

For a moment Anne thought he would argue, but then he shrugged and murmured, "As you wish."

They left shortly after that and back in the car Anne rested her head against the seat, eyes closed. It had been a very long day. Unable to sleep past seven, Anne had finally pushed the covers back and dragged her tired body out of bed. She was not sleeping well, and when she did sleep, her rest was broken by dreams. Wild, distorted dreams that made no sense and left her shaken and frightened. Most upsetting of all was the reoccurrence of the drowning dream she'd had the first night Jud was home. It was always the same, never varying, and that alone shook her. She had promised herself she'd sleep late that morning and the fact that she was unable to do so sent her to the breakfast table irritable and snappy.

Jud had been sitting at the table, his breakfast finished, drinking his coffee while his eyes scanned the morning paper. His "good morning" had been coolly polite and when Anne barely mumbled a response, one bleached brow went up mockingly.

"Fall out on the wrong side of the bed this morning, Anne?" His silky tone had irritated her even more. "Or is the boss running you ragged?"

"The boss," she emphasized scathingly, "hasn't seen the day he could run me ragged. I will be fine as soon as I've had some coffee."

Brave words. Too brave in fact, for he took her up on it at once.

"In that case I'm sure you'll be happy to join me for an hour or two in the library. I have a few questions on some legal papers of the old man's that I found in the desk. Perhaps you could supply some answers."

An hour or two, a few questions, the man was an expert at the understatement. He had grilled her endlessly, chiding softly "why not?" whenever she had to tell him she had no answer. He had had Mrs. Davis bring a lunch tray in to them and had given her barely enough time to finish her salad before firing questions at her again. By three thirty Anne was on the verge of tears, inwardly appalled at

69

how little she really knew of her stepfather's business affairs, when she'd thought she'd had a very good grasp of it all. Lord, if Jud could shatter her this soon, what in the world would he have done to the twins?

He had been studying a paper, head bent, when he calmly asked yet another question she had no answer for and in frustration she had almost screamed at him "I don't know." She'd paused, swallowing hard to force back a sob, then added chokingly, "I—I thought I had his complete confidence, but it's more than obvious I was wrong."

Jud's head had snapped up at her outburst and his eyes, those damned cat eyes, watched the play of emotions cross her face with cool intent. It was that watchfulness that drove her to turn away abruptly and head for the door. More unnerved than she'd ever been before, she'd whispered, "I—I'll understand if you want to replace me in the office, get another assistant."

She had reached the door, hand groping for the knob, when he grasped her by the shoulders, holding her still, her back to him.

"Throwing in the towel already, Anne?" he taunted softly. "I really thought you had more guts than to fall apart at the first obstacle. If you go, who is going to run interference for Todd and Troy?"

She had listened to his words in disbelief and when he'd finished, she'd gasped, "You mean you want me to stay?"

He shook her gently, then drawled, "My sweet Anne. Do you have any idea how long it would take me to train someone to replace you? I simply do not have the time. Besides which, I have known all along that you couldn't possibly know all of the old man's business. I was merely trying to ascertain exactly what facts you were cognizant of."

He'd hesitated, turned her halfway around to him, then stopped, dropped his hands, and stepped back, away from her. "You're tired," he snapped impatiently. "Take off and get some rest. You'll need it, for we still have one hell of a lot of work before us."

He'd walked away from her, the very set of his shoulders a dismissal. Anne had been only too happy to escape, for the touch of his hands on her arms had caused a feeling of extreme weakness in her legs, a tight breathlessness in her chest.

Anne moved restlessly against the plush covering of the car seat, then her eyes flew open as she felt the car slow down and then stop. Surely they couldn't be home already? They weren't. Andrew had brought the car to a stop on the side of a dark country road. He pulled the hand brake, then turned to her, an unfamiliar sheen in his dark eyes.

"Andrew, what—" that was as far as she got, for, without speaking, he pulled her into his arms and cut off her words with his lips.

At first Anne returned his kiss, but within seconds she was struggling against him, her hands pushing at his chest. This wasn't a kiss, this was an assault, and she went cold and unresponsive. Never before had Andrew kissed her in this demanding way and not questioning the feeling of revulsion that swept through her, Anne fought him frantically. Her struggles just seemed to add fuel to his fire and the pressure on her lips grew brutal, his teeth ground against her, bruising her soft mouth. She went stiff when his hand clutched painfully at her breast and in desperation she tore her mouth from his, cried out, "Andrew, have you gone mad? Let me go, please."

71

His breathing was ragged and uneven, his voice harsh as he released her, flung himself back behind the wheel.

"You don't give an inch, do you Anne?" His voice heavy with disgust.

Completely bewildered, Anne gasped, "I don't know what you mean."

"Don't you?" He almost snarled at her. "I'm human, Anne, a man. How long did you think I'd be satisfied with cold, chaste little kisses?"

"But—but you never said anything," Anne stammered.

"Good Lord, what do you suppose I was just trying to do? We've been engaged for three months. I have never considered a celibate existence. I need a woman and the woman who has agreed to be my wife has just turned away from me."

Overtired, overwrought, Anne stared at him, stunned. What could have caused this change in him? Not for one minute could she believe in his sudden overwhelming need of her. No, there was more to his about-face than that. But what could it be?

It wasn't until later, when she was safe in her own bed, that Anne realized Andrew had not actually said he needed her. That his exact words had been "I need a woman" not "I need you."

Even though Andrew had apologized after bringing her home, Anne begged off seeing him the following day. His attack—she could not even force herself to think of it as lovemaking—had left her feeling sick and in some way soiled, and for the life of her she could not think why. True, he had been rough, but she was a young woman and although she lacked actual experience, she was aware of the fact that there were times when men did get rough with women. She was going to be Andrew's wife, had known all along there would eventually have to be a physical side to their relationship. So why had she felt that revulsion, that near panic?

Anne spent all day Sunday unconsciously avoiding the answers to her own questions.

Her second week as Jud's assistant followed the same pattern as her first. Jud driving ahead tirelessly, Anne pushing herself to keep up with him. The only difference being that now she had an office of her own. It was there, she had seen it. She kept her handbag in one of her desk drawers but she was rarely ever in it. Also, in open defiance, she now left the building at lunchtime. If Lorna could go out for lunch, she'd asked herself angrily, why couldn't she? Her defiance was wasted on Jud, who merely glanced up when she'd informed him of her decision, smiled, and murmured, "Why not? It'll do you good to stretch your legs, clear out the morning cobwebs," and turned back to his work.

Although Anne had her doubts about the employer/employee status between Jud and Lorna, she observed no evidence to the contrary during the time Lorna was there. Their behavior was always office-procedure correct, her manner toward Anne respectful. Even so Anne breathed a silent sigh of relief when Lorna left the office early Friday afternoon, leaving Donna in possession of her desk.

Andrew called her several times during that week, but Anne put him off pleading either tiredness or work. Both of which were true, for Jud, having finished with the managerial files, had plowed into the mill employees folders. Anne found herself enclosed in the library with Jud most evenings, folders covering the large desk until, usually around nine thirty, her mother would rescue her with a softly chided, "Jud, really, you can't expect the girl to work all day

73

and all night. Why don't you both come into the living room, relax, and have a nightcap with me?"

Every night Jud's reaction had been the same. He had dismissed Anne at once, declined her mother's offer with a gentle, "Thank you, Margaret, but I want to give this a few more minutes. I would appreciate a drink in here though, if you don't mind." He would turn back to his work, giving Anne the impression that both she and her mother were immediately forgotten.

Friday night Anne and Jud were in the middle of a heated, though impersonal, argument concerning company policy on employee vacations when Mrs. Davis knocked quietly on the door and told Anne she was wanted on the phone. As Anne left the room Jud taunted softly, "Hold that last thought, because I'm prepared to destroy it completely."

Anger burning her cheeks, Anne snatched up the receiver and snapped, "Yes, who is it?"

"Hello to you too," Andrew replied, the very coolness of his tone causing the flush to deepen in her cheeks at her bad manners.

"I'm sorry, Andrew," she apologized quickly. "Jud and I were in the middle of an argument and I'm afraid I carried my impatience to the phone."

"You're not still working?" Andrew asked in amazement. "What in the hell is the matter with that man? Is it his goal in life to see you drop in your tracks?"

"Don't be silly," Anne soothed. "I'm sure Jud hasn't the vaguest idea of the number of hours I've put in the last two weeks. As to his wanting to see me drop in my tracks, I doubt he'd notice if I did. He'd probably just step over me and calmly go about the business of finding a new assisstant."

Andrew made a very impolite noise at his end, then said, "Not very complimentary to you. Try and break it up soon, will you, darling? We've been invited to a small dinner party at the home of a very important client tomorrow evening and I want you looking your best."

This sounded like the Andrew she knew and Anne wondered if he'd decided to ignore the incident of the previous Saturday.

"Anne?" Andrew's voice nudged.

"Yes, yes, of course. What time should I be ready?"

"We've been invited for pre-dinner drinks at seven thirty, so I'll come for you at seven. Will that be all right?"

"Yes, I'll be ready." Then a little devil inside made her tease. "And I promise I'll try not to disgrace you with my haggard appearance."

The teasing apparently went over his head, for he added, "I should hope not. As I said, this is a very important client."

Seconds later, as Anne cradled the receiver, she asked herself what had happened to Andrew's sense of humor, and realized, with a shock, that she'd never seen much evidence of his having one. Head bent, puzzling at her own lack of perception of the man she'd agreed to marry, Anne started back to the library. She had taken only a few steps when she was brought up short, her eyes encountering a pair of feet, one crossed negligently over the other. Slowly she lifted her head, her eyes following on an angle, long, jean-clad legs to slim hips and waist, a broad chest and shoulders, covered in a loose knit pullover and finally coming to an abrupt stop at two glittering amber eyes, the lids narrowed in amusement.

"Poor baby," Jud crooned softly. "Is the big, bad boss overworking you?"

Breathing deeply in a vain attempt to control her suddenly erratic heartbeats, Anne glared into those odd, felinelike eyes. Instilling a coolness she was far from feeling into her voice, she asked sarcastically, "Do you make a habit of eavesdropping on private conversations?"

Unabashed, unruffled, he leaned lazily against the door frame and allowed his eyes to roam slowly over her. When his eyes paused then fastened intently on her slightly parted lips, Anne had the weird sensation she could actually feel his hard, sardonic mouth touch hers.

Stifling a gasp, she stepped back, then stood still again as his soft laughter swirled around her.

"What are you afraid of, Anne?" Jud purred silkily. "You're as nervous as a prudish old maid at her first X-rated film."

Anger lent ice to her tone and covered her breathlessness.

"I am neither afraid nor nervous. I am simply too tired to play at words with you."

"Really? Then you'd better run along to bed, little girl." The purr deepened and slid along her skin like crushed velvet. "Do you want me to come along and tuck you in?"

Out of her league, and aware of it, Anne turned on her heel and started for the stairs, praying her shaky legs would carry her as far as her room. She had placed one foot on the first step when she paused again, her hand gripping the bannister, caught in that soft web.

"By the way, Annie, you can rest assured that should I ever find you sprawled at my feet, the last thing I'd ever consider doing would be to step over you."

Anne ran, his soft laughter chasing her all the way to her room. Safely inside, she dropped onto her bed, fighting the sudden, hot sting in her eyes. *What is wrong with you?* she lashed at herself impatiently. *Why do you let him upset you this way? He's deliberatly trying to undermine your confidence with his taunts and jibes, and you're allowing him to succeed by standing by meekly and taking it. Why? Why?*

Tired of the questions that seemed to have no answers. Anne undressed and went to bed, resigned to another restless night. It seemed she'd no sooner closed her eyes than they flew open again at the racket filtering into her room from the hall. Her room was flooded with bright, spring sunlight and, glancing at her bedside clock, she was surprised to find she'd slept the clock around. She felt good and a small indulgent smile curved her soft lips as she identified the cause of the upheaval in the hall. Todd and Troy were home for the spring break, bringing with them laughter and loud voices and all the attendant noises of youth.

"Cool it, you guys." The sharp command issued from down the hall came from Jud. "Your sister is still asleep and your mother doesn't want her disturbed. It's been a long two weeks."

It was wonderful to have the twins in the house again. Their constant banter, their incessant teasing, their forever dashing in and out, went a long way toward bringing a measure of calm to Anne's frayed nerves.

By Sunday night Anne faced the thought of going back to the office with much more composure than she'd left with on Friday.

She had enjoyed the dinner party she'd gone to with Andrew. And as he had seemed to have made another about-face, becoming once more the Andrew she'd always known, she found herself relaxing with him again.

That week Anne's work load in the office was somewhat lighter as Jud divided his time between the office and the mill, where he was overseeing Todd and Troy's training.

On Good Friday Anne and Jud worked alone in the office, the day being a legal holiday for employees. They worked steadily all day and by late afternoon Anne finally closed the last of the employee folders. Sighing wearily, she straightened and turned, then gave a softly gasped "Oh!" a second before Jud's mouth touched hers in a gentle kiss. It was over almost as soon as it had begun, and yet the havoc it created inside Anne was unbelievably intense.

"What was that for?" Anne whispered.

"That was a little reward for a job well done," Jud whispered back.

"Do—do you reward all your female employees that way?"

"You don't understand," Jud teased. "Your reward will be in your paycheck next week. The kiss was my reward."

CHAPTER

6

~

The weeks flew by. Busy weeks. Exciting weeks. The more Anne saw of Jud's business acumen, the more anxious she became for her brothers. She was way out of depth with Jud. Troy and Todd would have drowned in no time. Grimly she hung on, and yet she was loving every minute of it. Even the quarrels she had with him—and they were frequent—left her feeling tinglingly alive, if mentally exhausted.

By mid-April, one month after Jud took over, Anne faced the knowledge that she could not prevent him from doing what he wished with the company. His mind had absorbed all the information on the mill's management like a well-programed computer and that, along with his keen judgment of people, seemed to keep him three steps ahead of everyone else.

Anne had hardly been aware that spring had breathed life and growth back into the land until one evening as she drove home from the office. Suddenly it was all around her, the soft green of new grass and leaves, the elusive, sweet fragrance on the mild breeze, and the more mundane fact that she was uncomfortably warm in her suede jacket.

After parking her car Anne skirted around the garage and went into the yard behind the house. Slowly she walked along the flowerbeds, drinking in the scent of hyacinths, gently touching tulip and daffodil petals. After a complete circuit of the beds she sat down on the wrought-iron bench that encircled an old, gnarled apple tree. She had almost missed it, she mused wonderingly. She loved spring and she had almost missed it.

Sighing softly, she leaned her head back. What else had she missed since engaging in this battle of wits with Jud? She could not remember a single discussion she'd had with Andrew lately, or with her mother either. Had anyone mentioned how Troy and Todd were doing in school? She didn't know, hadn't known for weeks. Ever since Jud came home.

Jud.

Without warning tears filled her eyes, overflowed, and ran down her cheeks. Defenseless and vulnerable to the gentle tug of spring, Anne closed her eyes, made no effort to wipe away the tears. In rapid succession images flashed through her mind—Jud prowling the office, the library. Jud, hands on hips, taunting her, mocking her. Jud, gold hair glinting in the sunlight, a blaze of white teeth in a bronze face. Jud, amber eyes gleaming, watching—watching, and yet unable to see.

Jud.

With a small, strangled sob Anne lifted trembling fingers to her lips. He had kissed her on impulse to tease her. That had been weeks ago and still her mouth could taste the sweetness of his, feel its tenderness.

A wave of longing and raw hunger swept through her, washing away all pretense. Her hands covering her face, she sobbed hopelessly. She was in love with him again. No, she had never stopped being in love with him. And she was afraid. Afraid that one day those watching eyes would see and know.

A shudder tore through Anne's body and she sat up straight, eyes wide. The mere idea of Jud finding out how she felt made her go hot then cold. She had been so badly hurt by him ten years ago. She had never really stopped hurting, she admitted to herself now. She could not give him the chance to inflict deeper pain. Now her recurring dream of drowning in Jud's arms made somewhat more sense, for if he got even a hint of how she felt, he'd overwhelm her as surely as the water in her dreams did.

She would have to be very careful. Step lightly and cautiously if she was not to give herself away. It would not be easy. The results of the kiss Jud had dropped playfully onto her lips warned her of that. That meaningless kiss had rocked her world, left her trembling and yes—Anne admitted it—hungry for more. She wanted him and he was not for her.

A bitter smile curved fleetingly across her lips. No, he was not for her. And now, soul bared to herself at last, she identified the disquiet she'd felt every time Jud was out of town, as he was now.

Jud had told her, two weeks ago, that as his familiarization program was over he would spend at least two days a week in his New York office. Her disquiet had begun at that moment and had ballooned in size later that same day, when she overheard his phone call to Lorna informing her of his plans. Jealousy, pure unvarnished jealousy was eating away at her insides. That was the true name of her disquiet.

And he was there now, in New York with Lorna, and the thought of them together was tearing her apart. Visions of them swirled and formed in her mind. The tall, willowy redhead enfolded in Jud's arms, their mouths clinging, bodies entwined—on a bed.

A low moan of pain escaped through her lips and she felt nausea rise in her throat. The sound of her own voice startled her. *Stop it at once,* she told herself frantically. *How do you expect to get through the coming weeks if you fall apart every time you think of him with her?*

He had said, that first day, that he planned to stay a few months. One of those months was gone already, and somehow she had to make sure that when he did finally leave for good, he went away no wiser about her love for him than when he arrived.

The very thought of his eventual departure brought a flood of fresh tears to her eyes and she shook all over, as if with an illness. She jumped to her feet, and hurried toward the house. She had to get a hold on her emotions if she was not to betray herself.

Tears streaming down her face, Anne rushed through the back door, past an astonished Mrs. Davis and along the hall to the stairs. Her mother came out of the living room as Anne reached the stairs and at her ravaged face cried, "Anne, what in the world is wrong? Why are you crying?"

"Nothing, it's nothing," Anne choked. "I'm—I have a blazing migraine. I'll be all right if I can just rest for a while."

Margaret's anxious voice followed her up the stairs.

"But you've never been bothered with mi—"

Anne closed her door on her mother's words, stumbled across the room and flung herself onto her bed. Sobbing uncontrollably now, shattered, all defenses gone, she let the storm of weeping have its way.

Later, when the tempest had subsided to an occasional hiccupy sob, Anne lay staring at the ceiling, telling herself she was seven different kinds of a fool, one for each day of the week. And when her bedroom door opened, she didn't bother to turn her head, sure it was her mother.

"What caused the headache, Annie?"

Jud! It couldn't be. He wasn't due back until tomorrow. Gulping down an errant sob, Anne turned shocked eyes to stare at him. He stood by her bed, hands on his hips, every line of his body taut as if held still by a rigid control.

"Who knows what causes a migraine?" Anne hedged. Oh, Lord, just the sight of him was like a blow to her chest. Forcing a coolness she was anything but feeling into her voice, she flipped. "Don't concern yourself, these headaches usually disappear as fast as they appear."

"Can it, Anne," Jud growled. "Your mother informs me you've never had a migraine in your life. So what's caused you to fall apart like this?" His tone went low, fiercely demanding. "Has Andrew said or done anything to upset you?"

Andrew! Anne had the urge to laugh hysterically. Poor Andrew. At no time had Andrew had the power to shatter her in this way. Never had Andrew's nearness set off this chain reaction of breathlessness, trembling, warm flushes, and cold shivers.

Desperate to have him go, Anne shot back icily, "That's a personal question, Jud, and none of your business. You're the boss in the office, not here. Please leave my room. And don't ever come in here again without knocking."

His body went even more taut, his face set into grim, angry lines, and his eyes, through narrowed lids, seemed to glow with a burning intensity. Suddenly he moved, bent over her, and brushed a surprisingly gentle finger across the still damp hollow under her eyes. His voice was a frightening low snarl.

"If he's hurt you, I'll—"

Slim, cold fingers were placed over his lips, cutting off the intended threat. For brief seconds that seemed to stretch into eternity, cloudy gray eyes stared into angry amber.

"Annie."

The hard male lips moved against her fingers as he whispered her name. Tiny electrical shocks ran up her arm and through her chest to set her heart beating in crazy, pulsating thumps. Solid amber was melting to a soft liquid, threatening to absorb her will power. How very easily she could be lost in their depths. Her fingers moved across his smooth, hard cheek, delighting in the feel of him. His scent, a mixture of spicy aftershave and normal male muskiness, sent her senses spinning. She knew she should not be allowing this intimacy, she just couldn't remember why.

"Chicken."

The whispered word sent a screaming alarm through her mind. He had called her that ten years ago, then he had left her without a word, alone and hurt. How dare he accuse Andrew! She had to get him out of there before she made a complete fool of herself a second time.

Pushing at his chest with her other hand, she rolled away and off the bed on the other side. Eying him warily, her breathing ragged, she watched as he straightened slowly, his eyes steady on hers. The width of the bed between them gave her the courage to order. "Go away, Jud. You have no right to be here. I'm going to marry Andrew."

"Are you, chicken?"

Something in the tone of the softly spoken question made her uneasy, as if he knew something she didn't.

"Yes, of course I am." Anne rushed into speech in an effort to negate her unease. "Being left ten percent of the company stock has not tied me to the Cammerons for life. My plans are unchanged. I am going to marry Andrew."

To her amazement Jud stepped back as if she had struck him. Fleetingly a small, bitter smile twisted his mouth, then he turned and walked to the door. As he left the room his soft words reached her ears, confusing and, strangely, frightening her.

"I don't think so, honey."

Anne didn't go downstairs for dinner and she refused the tray her mother offered to send up to her. Sitting crosslegged in the center of her bed she stared vacantly at the wall, her mind darting wildly in an effort not to think of Jud.

No luck. Amber eyes seemed to glow inside her head and his soft voice taunted silently. *I don't think so. I don't think so.* Why not? Nothing had happened to give Jud the idea the relationship between her and Andrew had changed.

But it had changed! Anne frowned as the realization hit her. The blank look left her face, replaced by one of concentration. How had it changed? Being so busy the last few weeks she had seen little of him, and when they were together, she was tired and preoccupied. And yet it was more than that. Something about Andrew was different. Thinking back, Anne tried to pinpoint exactly when Andrew had changed. Uneasily she remembered that night she'd had to fight him off in the car. But that hadn't been the start of it, she had felt uncomfortable with him all evening. She cast her mind back further, to when he had left to go out of town before Jud came home. But no, the change had not yet started. He had told her he was sorry he couldn't be with her for the funeral and had kissed her, coolly and unemotionally. No, at that time he had been the Andrew she had always known. So when had the change started?

Then it struck her. Of course! The day he returned from that business trip, the day after Jud came home. Did Jud's return have something to do with the change in him? Surely Andrew didn't feel threatened by Jud. Anne puzzled at the thought a few minutes, then a new thought jumped into her mind. Jud's wasn't the only new face at dinner that night. Lorna? A picture of the beautiful redhead formed and with it one of Andrew, a surprisingly animated and attentive Andrew.

Ridiculous, Anne chided herself. Lorna had left weeks ago to go back to the New York office, and the change in Andrew remained. But then, she mused, Andrew's been going out of town on business more than ever before the last few weeks. Could there possibly be a connection? Come to think of it, he hadn't told her where he was going, or why. Could Andrew be interested in Lorna? Was there a man who, having met her, wasn't?

Wrong thought. Anne's mind veered to Jud. Jud, who had just that day came back from the New York office, and Lorna. Were they lovers? Anne moaned softly in protest against the searing pain the thought caused. Uncrossing her legs, she curled up on the bed, head cradled on her arm. Jud and Lorna. Jud with Lorna. Jud making love to Lorna. No. No. No. The pain grew inside as once again her mind filled with pictures of the two of them together.

Dear God, what was she going to do? How was she going to get through the coming weeks, working with him in the office, living in the same house? If he came near her, showed even the slightest concern, as he had earlier, she'd fall apart. She had so desperately wanted to feel his arms around her, have his mouth touch hers. A last, tiny bit of sense had saved her this time. But could she hold off against him if he should come that close again? Did she want to?

Her thoughts revolved around and around, always coming back to the same conclusions. She loved him, she wanted him, and, should he make a determined move toward her, she did not honestly know if she'd even try to repel him.

Andrew was forgotten. Lorna was forgotten. The only thing that remained was the stark realization that should Jud want her for any reason she was his. Anne sighed in defeat, she was his if he never wanted her.

It was an alarming thought and Anne closed her eyes tightly, giving in to the truth and the torment that truth brought with it.

I love you. I'll always love you. Long-ago words, returning to add to her torment. Anne felt she'd gladly give up another ten years of her life if she could hear those words again, feel the warmth of his body close to hers. Tears of regret slid silently down her cheeks. Why did it have to be Jud? Why couldn't she love Andrew this way?

Rolling onto her back, Anne wiped the tears from her face and stared at the ceiling. She'd have to break her engagement to Andrew. She couldn't marry him now, it would be unfair to both of them. But what was she going to tell everyone? What would they think? What would Jud think? Would he think about it at all? Or care? She doubted it. Jud was interested in only one thing—the company. That's what had brought him home and that was the reason he stayed. But he had set his own time limit. A few months he'd told Margaret. He'd been home over one month now and had completely familiarized himself with the management of the firm. A month or two at the most, Anne thought, and he'd be gone. Somehow she would have to get through those weeks with composure. She would have to play it very cool, for she was determined he'd leave as ignorant of her love for him as he'd arrived.

Anne finally slept, only to awaken several hours later shivering and scared. She had had that drowning dream again, only this time it was so clear, so real, she could still feel the coolness of the water, the heat of Jud's mouth. And, Lord forgive her, it would be worth drowning to be that close to him, if only for those few short moments.

Sanity returned with full wakefulness and Anne shuddered. *I must be cracking up,* she thought derisively. *The sooner that man goes back to his mistress the better. If he stays much longer, I'll be flinging myself into his arms and begging him to love me.*

It proved a lot easier to break her engagement to Andrew than Anne had dared hoped. That Saturday night they went to a small party at the home of one of Andrew's friends and surprisingly Anne enjoyed herself. It was the first time in weeks they'd been in the company of people their own age and as several of Anne's friends were there, there was no lack of conversation. The party was in the way of a double celebration—an engagement party and to celebrate the promotion of the newly engaged young man.

Anne observed the couple during the evening with something close to envy. They were so happy and so obviously in love. This is the way it should be, Anne thought sadly, her resolution to break her own engagement strengthening.

It was after two in the morning when they left the party and Anne, only half awake, barely heard what Andrew was saying until he said sharply, "Did you hear what I said, Anne? I'm leaving Slonne's office."

Fully alert now, Anne turned startled eyes to him. "But why? When will you go? Do you have another position lined up?"

"That's what I've been telling you for the last five minutes," he snapped exasperatedly. "I'm going into a very prestigious firm in Philadelphia. Tax work mainly."

"Philadelphia?" Anne was stunned, and it showed. "But Andrew, surely this hasn't happened overnight. Why haven't you told me before?"

For a moment Andrew looked uncomfortable, then he shrugged. "I wanted to be certain before I said anything. I accepted this firm's offer yesterday and told Mr. Slonne this morning. I'll be leaving in two weeks."

"Andrew," Anne hesitated, then plunged. "I think you'd better take your ring with you when you go."

The car was filled with silence for some time and Anne saw his hands tighten on the wheel then relax again. Sighing softly, in what Anne thought sounded very much like relief, he flicked her an evasive glance.

"I assume there's a reason you no longer want to marry me?"

This was the Andrew she had always known—cool, almost pompous.

"I just don't think it would work," she answered softly. "I'm sorry Andrew, But I'm afraid we're moving in different directions. Do you realize that tonight is the first time in weeks we've been with our friends? Whenever we go out it's in the company of clients or contacts. You're ambitious to the exclusion of everything else."

89

Andrew smiled cryptically. "Not quite everything, Anne."

Neither inclined or curious enough to question him on exactly what he meant, Anne rushed on. "I'm not saying that kind of ambition is necessarily wrong, it is just not for me." Anne paused, then honesty made her add, "Andrew, I don't love you. At least not enough to make a lifetime commitment to you."

They were almost home and Andrew was quiet as he drove up the driveway and parked in front of the large, old-fashioned house. His face somber, he turned to her, his arm resting on the steering wheel.

"You know, Anne, you've changed lately."

Anne felt a stab of pure panic. Had she given herself away? Then she sighed with relief as he added, "You always were quiet, but now, I don't know, you seem withdrawn and preoccupied. I suppose all the upheaval in the office hasn't been easy for you. You've really declared war on Jud, haven't you?"

"Andrew, it's not—"

"Never mind," he cut off. "You don't have to pretend with me. It's fairly obvious that you can't stand him. Don't misunderstand me, I don't blame you. I don't like him either, and I do understand you wanting to protect your brothers' interests until they're out of school."

He paused and Anne stared at him in wonder. Most of what he'd said after "It's fairly obvious you can't stand him," had barely registered. Fervently she hoped that everyone had the same impression of her feelings about Jud. Including Jud himself. Andrew's quiet voice intruded on her thoughts.

"As you've been honest with me, I think it only fair if I tell you I've been having doubts of my own about us."

Curious now, Anne had to ask, "Is there someone else, Andrew?"

He glanced away, then back again, a small, dry smile on his lips.

"Well, yes and no. I'm attracted to someone. I'm not sure if the attraction is mutual. I think it is, but I'm not sure. If you don't mind, that's all I have to say on it."

"No, of course I don't mind." Anne slipped his ring off her finger and handed it to him, adding, "Your private life is none of my business."

He looked rueful a moment as his fingers closed over the cluster of diamonds, then he shook his head once.

"No hard feelings, Anne?"

"No, Andrew, no hard feelings. I think we can be glad we realized our mistake now. It would have been much worse later. I will miss you though."

"I'm going to Philadelphia, Anne," he laughed softly. "Not the end of the world. If you need anything," he grinned, "like free legal advice, call me. Oh, by the way, I will still expect an invitation to Troy and Todd's graduation party."

"You'll have it." Leaning to him, she kissed him lightly on the cheek.

"Good luck, Andrew, with the new firm and—everything."

As luck would have it, Jud was the first to notice the lack of adornment on Anne's finger, and then it would have to be when they were all at the dinner table on Sunday, while Mrs. Davis was serving the soup.

"Your hand appears strangely naked, Anne," he drawled. "You haven't misplaced your engagement ring, have you?"

All eyes, including Mrs. Davis's, swung to Anne's

hand. Pink-cheeked, hating him, she snapped, "No, I haven't misplaced it; I gave it back."

"Anne!"

Her mother's shocked voice had Anne wishing she hadn't avoided everyone all day on the pretext of having things to do in her room. She had known she should go to her mother with some sort of explanation, but she had shied away from it. Now she was sorry she hadn't.

Anne drew a deep calming breath before saying quietly, "It's all right, Mother. I—I—Andrew and I—well, we've decided to call it off."

"But why? Anne, I don't understand." Margaret's voice held a plaintive note. "I don't understand you anymore. You're changing. Everything's changing." She sent a bitter glance at Jud, who received it with a look of total unconcern, before she went on, her voice rising an octave. "I seldom see you anymore." She glanced from Troy to Todd.? "I seldom see you two anymore. I feel like a stranger in my own home. And now this." Her voice rising even more, she turned again to Jud. "You, you said you would not disrupt this house, yet, since you came home, there's been nothing but disruption."

"Mrs. Davis, I think you'd better wait a few minutes before serving the rest of the meal. I'll call you when we're ready to resume eating." Jud's flat tone dropped into the silence that had gripped the room after Margaret's outburst.

"Yes, sir."

He waited until the door swished closed behind the housekeeper, then turned eyes as hard as flint to Margaret.

"Actually, Margaret, what I said was I had no wish to disrupt the normal routine of this house. I'm sorry if Troy and Todd's absence upsets you, but, as that is how it has to be, you may as well get used to it."

"Now look here, Jud, you—" Todd began.

"Don't interrupt," Jud snapped. "I never said there wouldn't be any changes. The old man indulged you, I won't. I haven't the time or the inclination. Margaret, you have no cause for complaint. In the last month I've paid bills for you to the tune of three thousand dollars."

Anne's eyes flew to her mother. What in the world had she bought? Her silent question was answered defensively by Margaret.

"I needed some new spring clothes, darker colors. I'm still in mourning for your father."

"I don't think the question of need applies here." Jud's tone was dry. "But that's beside the point. The point being, I have not questioned these expenditures. As stated, the bills are paid." One pale eyebrow was cocked in Troy and Todd's direction. "Yours too."

A frown creasing her smooth brow, Anne watched as a flush mounted in her brothers' faces. Good grief! Todd and Troy too?

But why? They received a more than generous allowance. This time Jud answered her silent questions.

"Don't delude yourselves into believing I don't know what the game is. The name of the game is Test Jud." Jud's eyes moved slowly around the table and the smile that twisted his lips made Anne's blood run cold. "There will be no more games, no more tests. Is that understood?"

Silence and three pairs of eyes guiltily turned to Anne with a mute appeal for help.

"Jud, really, I don't think there was any intention—"

"Shut up, Anne."

Anne gasped at the hard finality of Jud's tone. Who the hell did he think he was?

As if he could read her mind, Jud told her exactly who he was.

"I know what the intention was and I'm having no more of it. I made it perfectly clear at the beginning that I am the boss. I wasn't playing with words and I wasn't kidding. Now for the last time, is that understood?"

Anne found herself nodding her head in unison with the three he had addressed his question to. Awareness of the docile action brought a stillness to her body, a flare of anger to her eyes. Jud's sharp glance did not miss the flare and, as if in a deliberate attempt to fan it into a full flame, he prodded, "I haven't received any of your bills, Anne. Strange, but it would seemed that the only one of you that does any real work is also the only one not spending like a drunken sailor."

Anne's head snapped up, eyes now blazing.

"I pay my own bills," she stated emphatically. "I always have. As for Mother, Troy, and Todd, your father set the life-style by which they live. Why should it surprise or annoy you if they expect to go on as before? They know the money is there; and the company is doing very well. Dammit, Jud, you can't expect them to adjust to all these changes overnight."

"Ah—the champion jumps in to beard the lion." Jud's soft purr scraped like a rough file against Anne's anger. "Little mother to the rescue," he taunted. "I really hate to stamp on your act," he lied, "but I hardly think five weeks can be classified as overnight. I am not my father. It was his company solely. I have no intention of working myself into the grave just so my family can live in the same life-style. Not for forty-five percent of that company, or, for that matter, anything at all. There will be changes. Get used to it."

"As easy as that?" Troy snapped his fingers, his expression full of contempt.

"No, Troy, I didn't say it would be easy." Jud's words were slow and measured, each one underlined verbally. "But by the time you come into your own in the company, you'll know you've earned it. And believe me, that knowledge cannot be measured in time or money. Now, will it upset anyone if I suggest we finish dinner?"

CHAPTER

7

As she drove to work the following morning Anne had the feeling of being reprieved, if temporarily. The topic of her broken engagement had been submerged under the barrage of angry words that had been hurled around the room and Anne had escaped to her bedroom before it could be revived. She knew she would have to give her mother a fuller explanation, probably the minute she got home from work, but meanwhile she had the whole day in which to form the words plausibly, she thought.

When exactly was it that your brain stopped working? Anne asked herself ten minutes after she entered her office. That was right after Jud walked through the door from his office, stood, hands on his hips, in front of her desk and said bluntly, "You never did say why you and Andrew decided to call it off."

Damn the man. Anne held her breath a moment, then let it out very slowly. Why did he have to look so good? In a buff-colored suit and cream silk shirt he was tawny all over. Was he aware of the effect? Anne wondered. Very likely. Needing to put some distance between them, Anne pushed back her chair, stood up, and walked to the window, tossing over her shoulder, "I didn't realize I was obliged to say why."

"To me? Or anyone at all?"

Anne jerked at the sound of his voice right behind her. How in the world did the man move so silently? It was enough to give you the goose bumps.

"To anyone, really."

Her voice betrayed her shakiness and in defense she kept her head turned to the window.

"Annie, are you hurting?" he asked softly. "You sound on the verge of tears. And you were crying Friday night. Has he hurt you very badly?"

"It's nothing I won't live through," she murmured. Lord, how easy it would be, and how tempting, to let him believe it was Andrew she'd been crying over and who put the tremble in her voice now. But it wouldn't be fair to cast Andrew as the heavy. She would just have to bluff it out. Her voice stronger, she added, "I told you Friday I had a bad headache. I've had several lately. I guess I've been working too hard. As for Andrew, no, he hasn't hurt me. It was a mutual decision. We want different things from life, that's all."

"And it took you all these months to discover that?"

Jud's tone conveyed his disbelief and in desperation Anne cried, "Yes. I knew he was ambitious, but I didn't know how much so until just lately."

"There's something wrong with ambition?"

"No, no. Oh, you don't understand."

"I know," he replied quietly. "That's why I'm asking."

Exasperated, Anne spun around and went taut, her breath catching in her throat. He was so close she could see the dark brown flecks in his amber eyes, eyes that roamed slowly over her face, then settled on her mouth. Barely able to breath, Anne choked, "He—he no longer wants to socialize with anyone but

97

business contacts and he's leaving Mr. Slonne's office, going into a bigger firm in Philadelphia."

"So," Jud purred, "he finally landed it."

"What do you mean?" Anne whispered, eyes widening. "Did you know about this?"

"For several weeks now." Jud paused, studying her closely as if trying to decide whether to tell her more. Suddenly he shrugged in a why-the-hell-not sort of way and said, "Lorna's father is a senior partner in a very high class law firm in New York." He smiled slightly at the surprise on her face and chided. "Yes, Annie, Lorna doesn't have to work as a secretary. Not for me or anyone else. She chooses to do so. A smart girl is our Lorna. But that's beside the point. Anyway, not long after Lorna went back to New York, Andrew ran into her. He took her to lunch and during the course of conversation she mentioned her father. That was all your ambitious Andrew needed. Through Lorna he met some people, made some of those business contacts you just mentioned and, from what you've said, they have paid off. This move he's making is really for the best, Anne," he tacked on softly. "He would never have been content here."

Even though Anne didn't love Andrew and the engagement was irrevocably broken, she felt cheated and in some way betrayed. All this time he'd been seeing Lorna, making plans to change firms and he hadn't said a word to her. Why? Anne had no idea that her thoughts gave her face a wistful, lost look and the harsh tone of Jud's voice startled her.

"Forget him. You wouldn't have been happy with him anyway. You couldn't have given him what he needs."

"What?"

The tone and the words were like a slap in the

face, an insult to her femininity and the pain they caused laced her voice.

"Exactly what I said." The tone was softer, but the words just as hard. "Andrew is a man on the make. For position, power. He needs the kind of woman who's willing to keep up with him, if not one step ahead. The kind of woman who, if she doesn't have them already, will go out and make contacts and friends, who'll help him move up. You're not that kind of woman, Anne, and you'd tear yourself apart if you tried to be."

Andrew's words "I've been having second thoughts myself" were now very clear. He had reached the conclusion that she was not the right kind of woman. What kind of woman was she? Was she any man's kind of woman? She only wanted to be one man's kind of woman and it was obvious from the way they were always arguing that she wasn't that. The thought sent a wave of defeat through her and fighting tears she closed her eyes. The next moment her shoulders were being grasped and she was pulled roughly against a hard, exciting chest.

"Don't look like that," Jud rasped. "Dammit, Anne, there are other men in the world. Men worth one hell of a lot more than he is in all the ways that count."

Oh, Jud. There is only one man in this world I'll ever be able to see. Oh, God, I love you. If you knew what sweet torture it is to be held in your arms like this. Don't ever stop holding me. Don't ever go away again. Name your price and I'll pay it, whatever it is. Just don't leave me like you did before, hurting, longing, wanting.

The very intensity of Anne's emotions frightened her, made her draw back. *I have got to stop this,* she thought wildly. *If I don't clamp down on my feelings,*

I'll shatter like a piece of glass when he finally does go. Help me, Jud, she pleaded silently. *Insult me, fight with me. Anything, only please, please help me.*

Maybe prayers are answered, even silent ones, for at that moment Jud released her and stepped back, his fingers raking through his hair. His face seemed a little pale, his breathing not quite even as he prowled around the small room, then he strode into his own office, slamming the door behind him. A few seconds later the door was flung open again and he ordered, "Anne, come in here."

Anne smoothed clammy palms over her skirt, adjusted first her blouse, then her blazer, then, composing her face, walked as calmly as possible into his office. He was perched on the corner of his desk, the fingers of one hand drumming impatiently on the gleaming surface. A deep frown drew his eyebrows together and he had a unleashed, dangerous look.

"I know this is probably not the right time," he began quietly enough, "but I have to ask you something."

Completely mystified by his tone, she asked equally quietly, "What is it?"

He hesitated, not looking at her, then he turned the full blast of glittering amber on her.

"I want you to sell me your stock."

Stunned, Anne dropped into the chair in front of him. Was he out of his mind? Or did he think Andrew had so wounded her she would be grateful to sell out, creep away somewhere and lick her wounds?

"Sell you my stock," she replied dully. Then anger took over. "Jud, you know very well I won't do that!"

She moved to get up and his hard hands came down onto her shoulders, holding her in her chair.

"Wait, hear me out."

It wasn't a request, it was an order. From the boss

to the assistant. Anne threw him a mutinous look, but she made no further move to rise.

Jud went on the prowl, back and forth, around his desk, while Anne sat, her back straight as a yardstick, hands clasped tightly on her lap. Finally he came to a stop in front of her, fists jammed aggressively on his hips.

"I've got a deal in the works," he stated flatly. "A very large deal. It would mean a leap forward for this company. So far it's on simmer, but I know I can pull it off. It will give this company new life and we need it. But to do it I have to have control."

He stopped, waiting, his eyes hard and steady on hers, as if willing her to give him what he wanted.

Anne squirmed under that intense stare, longing to give him anything he wanted, knowing she dared not.

"What do you mean, we need it?" Anne began carefully. "We're not in trouble, our profits are good."

"We're stagnating." Jud's tone challenged her to deny his word. "With the rate of inflation our profits have remained static for the last few years. I've gone over the books, Anne. The old man was letting it drift. You can get away with that only so long. Nothing remains static, and the handwriting is on the wall for this firm. If we don't move forward, we'll slip back and once that starts, it's forget it."

Anne stared at him, unwilling to believe him, yet convinced he was right. If she had learned nothing else about him over the last month, she had learned one thing: In business matters Jud was thorough. But one point bothered her.

"All right, if you say we must make this deal, whatever it is, I'll believe you. But why must you have complete control? For all intents and purposes you are the head of the company. You have run things since the first day you stepped into this office. Why must you have a majority to close this deal?"

Jud sighed, then patiently, as though he were explaining something to a slow-witted child, he proceeded to enlighten her.

"First of all let me briefly outline what this contract would entail. Expansion, new machinery, a bigger work force. With what this company wants we'd need some new, innovative designers. They know what they want. It would be our job to produce the finished product."

As Jud warmed to his subject Anne could actually feel the excitement building in him. He had taken the bit between his teeth, now he was all set to run with it.

"We can do it, Anne," he finished forcefully. "I know we can do it." He paused then added softly, "And I want it."

"You still haven't explained why you must have my stock."

He frowned, then grimaced. "I would have thought that was self-evident. They won't go with me."

"They," Anne asked softly, "being the twins?"

"Who else?"

He turned away abruptly, his fingers raking through his gold-kissed hair. His tone, his actions, every taut line of his powerful body screamed his disgust at her.

"But why?" Anne cried, almost frightened by the restless, charged aura that surrounded him. "It would be to their advantage too, wouldn't it?"

"Hell, yes," he spun on her with very much like a growl. "But you are and have been aware of their attitude. They are in open revolt. So far in the short amount of time they have spent in the plant, they have made it their business to learn as little as possible about its actual workings. Oh," he snarled, "they have gotten to know a lot of people, have made a lot of friends. They are charming and easy to like, when they want to be. And the employees feel flattered that Judson Cammeron's sons have gone all out to be friendly." Jud's voice grew even thicker with disgust. "But, dammit, Anne, charm and friendliness doesn't keep the plant running, nor does it scrape together the payroll. In short, Anne, I have talked to them. And they've given me a loud, resounding no. Or, as our so charming Troy put it, 'we're doing fine as we are. Let well enough alone.' "

She should have known without asking. She really should have known. She was, as Jud had pointed out, very well aware of her brothers' attitude toward him. She was also aware of their ignorance in business matters. She had the very uneasy feeling that simply by asking she had set a match to a very short fuse. Keeping her voice low in an effort to dampen some of the fire raging inside him, she offered, "I'll talk to them. Make them see it would be advantageous to everyone if they went along with you."

"Terrific," he snapped sarcastically. "Problems solved. Dammit, Anne, they informed me—smugly—before they left to go back to school, that they will not be home again until after graduation. What the hell do I do in the meantime?"

Anne felt her own anger stir. Who did he think he was talking to, the youngest typist in the pool? Did he think she was that stupid?

"You negotiate, as you damn well know," she snapped back. "Graduation is only a few weeks away. I promise I'll speak to them at the first opportunity. There's more than enough time."

"And if there isn't?" Jud jibed. "What will you do then?"

He is deliberately pushing, trying to force a commitment from me, playing the odds that I don't know exactly how long a deal of this kind can take to close. Fighting down her mounting anger, Anne arched her eyebrows, widened her eyes innocently and smiled sweetly.

"Cry?"

Jud acknowledged defeat with a quick, rueful grin.

"Okay, you win. I was pretty sure you knew your job, but I had to take the chance." He shrugged, then his voice took on a no-nonsense edge. "But I'm not taking any chances with this contract, Anne. You had better be able to convince those two airheads on this, because I meant what I said last night. I'm through playing games. If they insist on fighting me I'll chew them up and spit them out."

The weeks that followed dragged interminably. Not since she'd been a little girl waiting for Christmas had Anne remembered time moving so slowly. She rehearsed and re-rehearsed what she'd say to Troy and Todd, and each new argument she came up with seemed more ineffectual than the last.

She fretted and worried and tried to hide from everyone, including herself, the deep, empty longing that enveloped her whenever Jud was away, which was most of the time. He had, he said, meetings to go to, conferences to attend, his New York office to check out and people to see. Including Lorna? Just the thought of the redhead twisted through Anne like a bent blade. Lord, she asked herself at least every other day, if she was like this now, what would she feel when he left for good? That eventuality didn't bear thinking about, so she didn't. Instead she concentrated on the twins, her work, her mother, the weather. Anything, anything but the pain in store for her.

But time did, as it always does, move forward and the day finally came for Anne and Margaret to drive upstate for Troy and Todd's graduation exercises.

Jud had been in New York for the last four days and when he sauntered into the dining room as Anne was finishing her breakfast she was so surprised she nearly choked on her toast.

"When did you get home?"

"Early this morning," he grunted.

Anne studied him from under her lashes as he walked to the swinging door to the kitchen and asked Mrs. Davis for orange juice, toast, and a pot of coffee. Then she quickly lowered her eyes to her plate when he turned back to the table. He looked tired and harassed and in a very bad humor, but even so, he was the best thing Anne had seen in close to a week and her eyes devoured him hungrily.

He was quiet until after Mrs. Davis had placed his breakfast in front of him and swung out of the room again; then he asked in the same low grunt, "What time are we leaving?"

Try as she would, Anne could not keep the astonishment out of her voice.

"You're going with us?"

As they had the day he came home, his eyes went over her with slow insolence, his expression putting her firmly in her place.

"My dear Anne," he purred silkily, "I think I had to remind you before that Troy and Todd are not your exclusive property. At the risk of repeating myself, they are my brothers too. And, yes, whether you approve, or not, I am going with you. Or rather you are going with me, as I'm driving."

"The Firebird?"

"No, I drove the Cadillac back. I thought it might come in handy if the twins want us to lug some of their junk home for them. That's why I didn't get back last night. I cancelled my plane reservation and left New York soon after midnight."

Anne wasn't sure she could believe what she'd heard. Jud explaining his actions to her? He must be even more tired than he looks, she reasoned.

"I didn't know you had a Cadillac. Or isn't it yours?"

The minute the words were out Anne wished them unsaid. She had no right to pry into what was and was not his and she waited for his verbal slap down. Strangely it didn't come. Instead, Jud refilled his coffee cup, leaned back in his chair, took a sip, then, with a small smile playing at the corners of his mouth murmured, "Yes, Anne, it's mine. It's a gas guzzler of course, so I don't drive it very often. Most of the time it just takes up space in the parking garage at my apartment building. I've considered either selling it or bringing it here, but I haven't decided just what I want to do with it." He paused, then added seriously. "You wouldn't want to use it, would you? That car of yours looks like it has about had it. You're welcome to it, if it takes your fancy."

Tired! The man must be near unconsciousness. Unable to resist taking advantage of his sudden mellowness, Anne teased. "No, thank you. But if you want to keep it here and drive it yourself, I'll gladly run the Firebird for you."

"You like the Firebird?" Pale brows went up in question.

"Of course I like it," Anne laughed. "It's a super hunk of machinery, and you know it."

"All right, I'll leave the Caddy here and use it myself." He shrugged. "You can have the Firebird."

He meant it! He really meant it!

"No! Jud, really, I couldn't." Flustered, Anne's

106

words tripped over one another. "I didn't mean—I mean I was only teasing—I couldn't take your—"

"Anne, be quiet," Jud sighed. "I know you were only teasing. But I wasn't. I don't trust that heap you drive."

Anne opened her mouth to argue, then closed it with a snap when he chided, "And don't go all moralistic on me. I'm not making you a gift of the car, simply putting it at your disposal. The car will be here, you have my permission to use it, that settles it."

"That settles what?"

Margaret followed her question into the room, her eyes studying Anne's flushed cheeks before swinging to Jud.

"I've just been telling Anne that since I brought my other car back with me, she may as well make use of the Firebird, retire that pile of scrap she drives."

"About time too," her mother agreed promptly. "I've been after her for over a year now to buy a new car. I don't think the one she has is entirely safe."

"Mother," Anne sighed in exasperation, "I told you I'll get another car when I can afford it. My car is not all that bad; it passed inspection, you know. Besides which, I can't use Jud's car, I'd be too afraid of something happening while I had it."

"Don't be silly, dear," Margaret brushed aside her argument. "You are an excellent driver and I really think you should accept Jud's offer."

Anne fumed and stared icicles at Jud, who sat back lazily in his chair, a look of smug complacency on his face.

"Mother," Anne breathed angrily.

"Now, Anne, please don't go on about this. As Jud said, it's settled." The subject closed as far as she was concerned, Margaret calmly poured herself coffee.

Simmering, not daring to look at Jud, afraid that if

she did and he still wore that self-satisfied expression she'd throw something at him, Anne spoke through clenched teeth.

"What time would you like to leave, Mother?"

Margaret glanced casually at her wristwatch, then answered calmly, "In a half hour."

"A half hour!"

Two outbursts, one male, one female, as both Anne and Jud jumped out of their chairs. As she went out of the room, Jud at her heels, Anne heard her mother laugh softly.

"Do hurry, children. We'll have to stop for lunch on the way, and you know how I dislike rushing through a meal."

Unbelievable, Anne thought in wonder, as she rushed up the stairs. Apparently even her mother was not immune to the electricity Jud generated, or to his brand of humor either.

"Anne."

Jud's voice stopped her as she reached her door. Anne turned, impatient words hovering on her lips, but all that came out was an angry "Oh," for she saw a set of car keys dangling in front of her face, and two amber eyes glittering with steely purpose.

"Why don't you give in gracefully, Anne? Take the keys."

He is so sure of himself, Anne raged inwardly. *So damned confident he's won.*

"You know what you can do with your keys."

Spinning around, she grasped the doorknob just as his other arm shot out and his hand was placed flat, fingers spread, on the door panel.

"You're not getting in until you take the keys." His voice was a quiet taunt. "Better hurry, Annie, time's a-wastin'."

She didn't want his damned car. She didn't want

anything from him, but the one thing he couldn't give her. Her anger way out of proportion to the situation, Anne turned, sputtering, "You—you have no right insisting I use your stupid car. You have no right insisting I do anything. Take your hand away and let me . . . Oh!"

His blond head was lowered, and his lips, very close to hers, murmured, "There is only one way to calm a stormy woman."

Her protests were smothered by his mouth, in a kiss Anne felt certain he had meant to bestow lightly. But suddenly he groaned deep in his throat and his arms crushed her against the hard length of his body, his mouth fastened greedily on hers, demanding a response she had no will to refuse.

If only time could stop right here, right now, Anne mused dreamily, allowing her arms to coil up and around his neck, her fingers to slide possessively through his golden mane.

Anne could have remained locked within his arms for the rest of her life, but the old grandfather clock, which had stood in the foyer for as long as she could remember, struck the half hour and brought Anne to her senses.

Pulling away from him, she husked, "All right, I'll take your damned keys. But will you please let me go, we've only a few minutes."

His arms seemed unwilling to release her, his eyes held a strange, moody look and his face was a study in conflict.

"Anne, Annie—wait—I . . ."

Sure he was going to apologize, and not wanting to hear it, Anne pushed gently against his chest.

"Jud, please. We have got to get moving. Mother will have six fits if we are not downstairs when she's ready to leave."

109

Right on cue, her mother's voice floated up the stairs to them.

"Anne, Jud, why are you standing around the hall talking? Do you realize what time it is?"

With an impatient grunt, Jud dropped his arms, grimaced, then strode down the hall to his room.

Much to Anne's surprise, the drive upstate was pleasant and in the plushy, luxurious El Dorado, very comfortable.

At first conversation was minimal as Anne made a pretense of admiring the scenery, Jud concentrated on his driving, and Margaret, ensconced on the backseat, sifted through the small stack of mail she'd picked up from the hall table as they left the house.

"Oh, Jud, here's a note from Melly," Margaret murmured after some twenty-five minutes of total silence. "She says that as Franklin is doing so well now she'll be able to come up for the twins' celebration."

Melly was Melinda Cammeron Stoughten, Judson Cammeron's twin sister and Jud, Troy, and Todd's only aunt, which was one more than Anne had.

"Yes, I know," Jud answered quietly. "I spoke with her a few days ago. I was going to tell you, but it slipped my mind."

"How is Franklin, really, Jud?" Margaret asked anxiously. "It was so hard on Melly to lose her—" she faltered, then went on, "her brother, so soon after waiting through that horribly long operation on Franklin, being unsure for days if he'd live. I know that it tore at her heart not to be able to attend Judson's funeral, but it was impossible for her to leave Franklin at that crucial time."

"Yes, it was a hard time for her." Jud's voice had gentled to a loving softness. "I was with her the day before the funeral and she was in pretty bad shape.

As you know, like a lot of twins, Dad and Mel were on the same wavelength."

Turning her head to stare out the window at her side, Anne fought to control her trembling lips, the tears stinging her eyes. She had become resigned to him referring to his father as the old man, even though her mother still winced when he did, but now, not only had he said Dad, he'd said it in a tone that revealed to her some of the pain losing his father had inflicted. Anne ached for him, for the right to comfort him, and she ached for herself too. His expression had been so tender, so full of loving warmth. If he could look like that for a much-loved parent and aunt, what would he be like with a woman he was in love with?

Anne blinked rapidly as an errant thought stabbed her mind. Was Lorna the recipient of his loving glances? She had seen no evidence of it while the beautiful redhead had been in the office, but that meant little. Both Lorna and Jud were too intelligent not to be circumspect in a business atmosphere.

Jealousy, pure and simple, consumed every fiber of Anne's being and along with it an emotion both alien and frightening. Hate—ugly, soul-destroying hate for Lorna—tore at her mind so viciously she had to clamp her lips together to silence a snarling moan.

This can't be happening to me, her mind screamed in protest. *I can't let this happen. I feel like I'm losing my mind and I can't bear it. What I feel for him can't be love. Love is suppose to be a tender emotion, overflowing with compassion and understanding. If I loved him, really loved him, I'd want his happiness more than anything else, even if that happiness could only be achieved with someone else. But I don't feel that way,* she cried in silent anguish, *what I feel is totally selfish. I want to be the one he reserves his most*

111

*loving glances for; I want to be the one he hurries to
when he leaves his office, and I want to be the only
one he can't wait to have in his arms, in his bed.*

Unnerved, scared stiff by the raw intensity of her
thoughts, Anne forced her attention to Jud's quiet
voice. He was still discussing his aunt and uncle with
her mother—could it only be a few minutes that she'd
burned in the hell of her own emotions. In desperation she grasped at the threads of their conversation.

". . . that was two weeks ago," Jud said calmly.
"But when I talked to her the other day she said his
improvement had been so great they think they'll be
able to dispense with the live-in nurse within a few
weeks."

"Oh, I'm so glad, Jud." Margaret sighed softly, her
gentle heart touched by her brother-in-law's suffering.
"I wish she could stay longer than one day, although
I can fully understand her wanting to get back as
soon as possible. I truly like your Aunt Melly, Jud.
I always have."

"So do I." Jud laughed softly, then added seriously,
"I know you do, Margaret. And I also know the
feeling is returned." Then, as if to lighten the serious
mood, he added, "I also wish she could stay longer
than the one day. Mel is so full of life and joy herself,
she seems to infuse it into everyone she comes into
contact with."

The conversation drifted easily into more general
subjects and Anne, though adding little, hung on to
every word as to a lifeline. The balmy weather was
discussed, and the beauty of the rolling Pennsylvania
countryside on which spring had once again settled itself so gracefully.

Turning her head dutifully to observe the yearly
phenomenon, Anne's eyes were caught then held by
two horses running across a white-fenced paddock.

The stallion was large and as he pranced along he alternately tossed his beautiful, regal head and nipped playfully at the daintily dancing mare at his side. Anne heard a low chuckle beside her, then she winced as Jud murmured, "Go get her, big fellah."

CHAPTER

8

Even with the graduation exercises over and the twins, with all their assorted belongings, home again, Anne could not get them together in one place long enough to have any kind of serious discussion. They were too busy with the hours they put in at the mill, settling in at home, and getting things organized for their party at the end of the week to go into a conference, they insisted.

Jud was beginning to positively scowl at her and, as if that were not enough, she was facing a problem that worried her more than a little.

The problem, in the form of John Franks, showed up the day after the twins' graduation. Why he was there was self-explanatory, for Jud was methodically feeding him information about the textile business. Why his presence at and understanding of the company was necessary at all was what worried Anne.

Questions tormented her every waking hour, the main one being Was Jud training John to replace her?

About the same age as Jud, John Franks was a good-looking, easy-going man whose demeanor belied his sharp mind. He had taken Anne to lunch a few times, on the occasions when he'd been in town negotiating for Jud with Mr. Cammeron, and Anne liked him very much. He had been amusing and entertaining and had not stepped out of line once.

On his first day at the office he had looked pointedly at Anne's third finger and, eyebrows raised slightly, said, "The fool surely didn't let you get away?"

"No getaway necessary, John."

Anne's reply was made without strain. She had always been easy and relaxed in John's company. Then in a gently scolding tone, she added, "And Andrew is not a fool, John."

"Couldn't prove that by me," he retorted amiably, seating himself on the corner of her desk. "Personally, I thought he was not too bright in not rushing you to the altar the minute you said yes."

"Of course," Anne laughed lightly. "Words of wisdom from a man I strongly suspect is a confirmed bachelor."

"Only because, by the time I met you, you were already spoken for."

John's words were spoken in such earnest, Anne felt the laughter die in her throat. Before she could form a reply, Jud's voice drawled from the doorway.

"If you can tear yourself away from my assistant, John, I'd like to get down to work."

John's fair cheeks flushed a ruddy hue and his eyes flashed warningly as he turned to face the doorway.

Jud's stance, with his shoulder propped against the door frame, was the only indolent thing about his appearance. Pale eyebrows arched arrogantly over two glittering chips of amber stone, his face set firmly and his lips were twisted in the now familiar sardonic slant.

Obviously on the verge of an angry reply, one look

at Jud seemed to change John's mind, and with a mild shrug he murmured, "You're the boss, Jud."

"I know."

Jud's silky purr had the same effect on Anne as an ice cube being drawn down her spine. Biting her lip to keep from shivering, Anne stood mutely as Jud stepped aside to allow John to walk by him into his office, then, his smile mocking, Jud pulled the door to, closing John in, shutting her out.

Saturday, the day of Troy and Todd's party, dawned bright and warm, perfect weather for a party that would, in all likelihood, spill out of doors.

Anne found herself on the move from the moment she finished her breakfast. Suddenly her mother discovered half a dozen errands for Anne to run and she was kept too busy to think, dashing around in the Firebird.

Jud absented himself from this frenzy of activity until lunchtime. Anne, her mother, Troy, and Todd had started their meal, thinking Jud would not show up, when he strode into the room, a very reluctant-looking John at his heels.

Jud waved John to a chair, seated himself, and favored Margaret with a charming smile.

"As John is on his own here, I insisted he join us. Not only for lunch, but for the bash tonight as well."

Without batting an eyelash, Margaret returned his smile with one of equal charm.

"Well, of course he must stay." She then turned the smile on John.

"I'm sorry I didn't issue the invitation myself, John, but I've been so busy the last few days. I'm sure you'll understand."

John hastened to assure her he did, while Anne pondered on the changed relationship between her mother and Jud. She had no idea what she'd missed in the conversation the day they'd driven to commencement exercises, but whatever it was had caused the cessation of hostilities. The baffled expressions on the faces of her brothers told her they were even more mystified than she was.

With everyone on their best behavior in front of John, lunch was a pleasant, if brief, respite from the bustle. But from the moment they left the table Margaret began issuing orders like a field marshal and this time even Jud did not escape.

On her way from yet another trip between the kitchen and living room, Anne's arm was suddenly grasped and she was pulled unceremoniously into the library. Hearing the door close with a soft click, she turned and saw Jud leaning against it, a furtive look on his face.

Anne opened her mouth to ask what he was up to, then closed it when he placed a long forefinger to his lips and breathed a soft "Shush" as he pushed himself away from the door and came toward her. He didn't stop when he reached her, but kept on going, taking her with him with a firm hand placed in the middle of her back. When, at the far end of the room, he finally did stop, she spun on him.

"Jud, what in the devil—"

"I had forgotten what an organizer your mother is," he interrupted in a stage whisper. "Maybe I should put her to work somewhere in the company."

"Jud," Anne sighed warningly.

The teasing light left his eyes and he smiled ruefully.

"I wanted to talk to you, obviously." Jud's tone had changed from that of conspirator to one of control. "When the hell are you going to talk to Troy and Todd? I can't keep dodging around these people indefinitely, you know."

117

"I know, and I'm sorry." Anne raised her hands placatingly as Jud frowned. "I haven't been able to get them alone for longer than three minutes since they got home. I was hoping to corner them tomorrow sometime."

"Don't hope, do it," Jud ordered. "And I want to see you in here the minute you have." He paused, then added resignedly, "Now I suppose we had better get on with Margaret's craziness before she sets the bloodhounds on our missing trail."

By mid-afternoon all the preparations were completed to Margaret's satisfaction and Anne gratefully fled to her room to have a hasty shower and change of clothes before the guests began descending on them.

She spent more time than she really should have getting dressed, wanting, for some unobvious reason, to look her best. Finally finished, she stepped back from the mirror and critically surveyed her reflection. She had bought the dress she was wearing on impulse, and now was somewhat amazed at the vision before her eyes. The rich apricot chiffon set off her dark hair to perfection and gave a glow to her smooth pale skin. The scooped neckline revealed just a hint of a curve at her breasts, while the snug bodice outlined the enticements it covered. The sleeves were pleated and full as was the skirt, which swirled around her slender legs when she walked.

Giving a nod of satisfaction to the young woman in her mirror, Anne smiled and left her room. As she hurried down the stairs, the sound of voices drifted to her from the living room; one in particular brought a glow of pleasure to her eyes.

Melly had arrived and it seemed everyone was talking at once. Hanging back, Anne watched Jud's aunt as she laughingly replied to their questions. Tall and

118

slim, still lovely, Melly seemed to be plugged into the same high voltage circuit that Jud was, for she charged the air around her as forcefully as he did.

Within minutes of her entering the room, Anne saw Melly's and Jud's eyes meet in understanding and communication and felt a small stab of envy of the older woman.

"Anne, darling, why are you hovering there in the background?" Melly's soft, melodious voice chided. "Come here, dear, and let me look at you."

"Hello, Melly. You look wonderful, as usual."

Anne walked across the room and into the arms of the older woman, who then stepped back and let her eyes run quickly over Anne's small frame.

"Anne, I don't know how you manage it. But I swear you grow more lovely between my visits." Then Melly's eyes narrowed slightly and she sent a sharp glance at Jud. "Jud, are you working this child too hard? If she gets much thinner she'll float away on the air."

"Really, Melly—" Anne began, only to have Jud cut in.

"Anne has been working very hard the last month or so, Mel. But not to worry, I'm working on an arrangement now that will give her more free time."

Jud's tone was casually teasing, yet Anne felt suddenly chilled. What arrangement was he working on? Were her suspicions correct? Had John Franks been brought in to take over her job? Pushing the questions away, she made herself join in the conversation. This was her brothers' celebration, she would not spoil it for them by letting her worries show. All the same she decided to stay away from Jud as much as possible that evening.

The guests began arriving, and within the hour the house was filled with laughing people. While Jud, at

119

Margaret's side, played the host, Anne circulated around the room, greeting people she knew, meeting people she didn't, making sure no one went long without a drink or something to eat.

The house became steadily more crowded and, as the one half of the large double living room had been cleared of furniture, quite a few of the young people were dancing. As Anne had suspected, the less physically inclined drifted out through the french doors onto the side patio. The evening was warm and still, the scent of first roses heady, but Anne barely noticed as she moved around—avoiding Jud—making numerous trips between the living room and the dining room to keep an eye on the food supply.

Anne was returning from one of these buffet checks when the sound of new arrivals brought her head up sharply. Stepping back into the shadow of the stairway, Anne stood perfectly still, hands clenched, observing the group of people talking in the foyer.

Although she couldn't hear his words, Andrew's cool precise voice was unmistakable, as was the throaty laugh of the woman on his arm. Lorna, here! And with Andrew! Margaret's voice was a low murmur as she greeted the couple and the twins stood, just looking at Lorna, idiotic grins on their faces. At that moment Jud strode into the foyer from the living room hand outstretched to grasp the slim, white-gloved one extended to him. He said something softly that brought a dazzling smile to the redhead's face, then nodded coolly to Andrew.

Anne stayed where she was several minutes after the group had moved into the living room, eyes closed, breathing deeply to regain her composure. Damn him! Damn him for inviting her here. Anger surged through her and she thought bitterly, *He hasn't been to New York in almost a week, couldn't he bear being away from her any longer? And what was she doing with Andrew? Had they become such close friends she could ask him to escort her to the home of her lover?*

Just thinking the words made Anne feel ill, and for a fleeting second she considered running to her room. Fierce pride made her reject the idea. Squaring her shoulders, she formed her lips into a bright smile and headed for the living room. She hesitated a moment in the doorway, then saw two men moving toward her from opposite directions. Jud advanced from the left, his face set in grim determination, and from her right John approached, a smile of warmth lighting his face.

Not wanting to be anywhere near Jud, let alone talk to him, Anne walked quickly to meet John, seeing Jud stop dead out of the corner of her eye.

"Come dance with me." John smiled coaxingly. "You've been busy long enough. Time you relaxed and enjoyed the party."

Pliantly Anne allowed him to draw her into the cleared area, and into his arms. The music was slow and dreamy and as John turned her to him she caught a glimpse of Jud. He stood taut and angry where he'd stopped, his eyes hard and cold. Turning her head away, Anne was filled with fiery resentment. What right did he have to be angry? If she chose to dance with John instead of greeting Jud's lady-love, why should it bother him?

With a concentrated effort she pushed Jud from her mind and gave full attention to the dance. She loved to dance, had in fact, taken several classes in modern dance and she found John a polished partner.

"Hey, you're very good!" John's surprise amused Anne. "I should have dragged you onto the floor sooner."

"Thank you, kind sir," Anne laughed up at him as the music ended. "You're pretty good yourself."

The young man who had taken over the stereo must have decided it was time for a change, for the record that dropped onto the turntable was upbeat, the tempo fast and inviting.

Anne felt the beat in every muscle and agreed eagerly when John murmured, "Are you game?"

Within seconds Anne realized that John was not only good, he was very, very good, and Anne gave herself up to the enjoyment of the intricate, somewhat sensuous movements of the dance. As John moved beside her, at times spinning her away from him, then, one arm coiling her back close to his body, she became aware that the other dancers had moved back, leaving them in sole possession of the floor.

When the music stopped there was a burst of applause and several calls of "one more time."

Shaking her head, laughing and pink with embarrassment, Anne walked off the dance area.

"That was fun." John's arm, still around her waist, tightened. "Will you dance with me again later?"

"We'll see." Anne hesitated, then added ruefully, "But definitely not as the evening's entertainment."

Glancing around, she saw Jud again moving toward her and with a hurried, "Excuse me, I must go check on the food," she slipped out of the room.

Moving quickly, Anne went through the dining room, casting a cursory glance at the buffet, and on through the kitchen and out the back door. The enclosed garden at the back of the house was quiet and very dark. Not stopping until she was at the very back of the garden, Anne stood trembling with reaction. Jud's face had been so hard, his eyes blazing with fury. The brief glance she'd had of him before

122

she'd fled had filled her with something very much like panic.

"Who are you hiding from, Salome?"

The softly sardonic words coming out of the darkness startled Anne so badly she jumped, and with a gasp she turned on her tormentor.

"I'm not hiding from anyone, Jud. I just wanted some fresh air." Fighting to control her trembling breathlessness, she snapped, "Why did you follow me? What do you want?"

"I followed you because I'm curious." The disembodied voice blended into a blurred form as Jud stepped closer to her. "What exactly was that performance on the dance floor for? Was it simply a come-on to John? Or were you trying to get at Andrew by showing him what he'd given up?"

The suppressed rage in Jud's tone sent an arrow of fear zinging up Anne's spine and in an effort to hide it from him she laughed lightly, if a little shakily.

"Maybe a little of both." She heard his sharp intake of breath and added impishly, "Do you think it was effective?"

The next instant she was wishing she'd held her tongue, for his hands grasped her arms and pulled her hard against his chest.

"I think," he gritted through clenched teeth, "there was not a man in that room who didn't feel the effect. Myself included."

His hands loosened their painful hold on her arms, only to move up to clasp her face tightly.

"There are times, little girl, when you infuriate me." He drew her face so close to his she could feel his breath against her skin, could smell the fumes of the drink he'd had. "Then there are the other times, like now." His tone had dropped to a low rasp that sent tiny darts of excitement into her nerve ends.

"What do you mean?" she whispered.

"The answer to that is the same as the answer to what I want."

His mouth was almost touching hers and Anne felt a shock ripple through her when the tip of his tongue touched her upper lip.

"I want what was offered to me ten years ago," he murmured huskily. "I want what should have been mine before any other man's."

Anne gasped and would have denied his inference, but he wasn't finished, for he added harshly, "I want you."

His mouth crushed hers, his lips forcing hers apart, while his hands moved from her face to her back to pull her roughly to him. Struggling was futile as his arms tightened, holding her still, and as his kiss deepened she gave up the pretense. With a soft sigh she relaxed against him, savoring the possessive sweetness of his mouth. As her body softened, his seemed to grow harder, the muscles in his arms, shoulders, and thighs tautening in urgency. His mouth released hers, slid slowly across her cheek.

"Annie, chicken, come with me now," Jud urged.

"Come? Where?"

"Anywhere," he husked. "My room. Your room. The car. I don't care as long as I can have you to myself awhile."

"But, Jud, we can't. We have a house full of people. Andrew, John, Lo—"

"The hell with Andrew and John," he gritted savagely. "The hell with all of them."

His mouth caught hers again, sensuously, lingeringly, until he felt her begin to tremble. His hand moved slowly over her ribcage, then her breast. Her small gasp was smothered by a swift hard kiss.

"Annie, honey, come with me to my room," his

124

softly purring voice enticed. "I don't care anymore what happened before. I don't care about Andrew or any others that may have been before him."

In between the whispered words his lips had moved over her face, down the side of her neck to explore the hollows at the base of her throat, while his fingers caressed and teased the growing fullness of her breast. Almost beyond sanity, on the verge of agreeing to anything he wanted, Anne felt a chill spear through her with his last words.

"Jud, you—"

"I think you'll find," he continued as if she hadn't spoken, "I'm just as competent at pleasing you as they were. You may even find I'm better."

The chill nosedived into a frigid cold and, not unlike the first day in his office, she pushed at him, tore herself out of his arms. Hurt and angry, Anne was past caring what she said.

"You overbearing clown," she snapped furiously. "Are you trying to drive me away?"

"Anne, what the hell—"

"If you are," she interrupted, "you don't have to humiliate and insult me to do it. Tell me you want me to go and I will. Gladly."

She moved to walk around him, but he caught her at the waist, pulled her so hard against him the breath was knocked out of her body.

"Andrew was not your lover?"

Strangely his tone was soft.

"That's none of your business," she hissed.

"Answer me, Anne."

A command, Jud was again the boss.

"No." Her voice was low, but emphatic.

"After being engaged for three months? I find that a little hard to believe."

Anger mounting, Anne struggled to free herself,

but his arms tightened to make her sure he'd crack her ribs if she moved.

"I don't give one damn what you believe," she whispered harshly. "Andrew never made love to me. And there were no others."

Although his hold did not loosen, he went completely still, not even seeming to breathe, then his breath relaxed in a long, slow sigh.

"It seems I owe you an apology again."

"Keep your apologies," Anne replied wearily. "They come too fast and glib after your insults."

"Annie, I said I was sorry. I mean it." The purr was back in his voice and against her will Anne felt her anger dissolving. "I wasn't trying to insult or humiliate you. Good Lord, woman, I know myself and had I been Andrew you would not have been able to answer no."

"Anne—Jud, are you out here?" Todd called from the back of the house. "Anne, Mother's looking for you, and Jud, Lorna's looking for you."

Anne stirred feebly against him.

"Jud, we must go—oh!"

His mouth touched hers, then covered it fully in a short tender kiss. As he lifted his head, he murmured, "Don't be angry with me, little girl. For if you're angry, you won't let me kiss you. And I sure as hell don't want that."

Flustered, Anne could find nothing to say and with a soft laugh he released her, all but her hand which he grasped firmly until they reached the back door.

The rest of the evening was a confused blank for Anne. Unable to erase the feel of Jud's mouth, his arms, and his perplexing words, Anne laughed and joined the conversation and could not remember afterward a single word that was said.

* * *

Anne slept late and woke to a June morning dark and overcast with storm clouds. Praying the weather was not a harbinger to what the day had in store for her, she went in search of the twins.

She found them at the breakfast table, slightly hung over, discussing the party desultorily. Receiving only nods and grunts to her bright "Good morning" Anne seated herself and picked at her breakfast in silence. When Todd and Troy left the table and headed for the stairs, she slipped out of her chair and followed them. When she reached the door to her room, they were a few steps ahead of her and she called softly, "Troy, Todd, I want to talk to you."

"Oh, Anne, must it be now?"

"Later, maybe, I have a rotten headache."

"I'm sorry, but it can't wait any longer." Turning the knob, she pushed the door open and, before they could object further, she nodded her head at the room. "Now."

They grumbled something about bossy older sisters, but they followed her, Troy dropping onto her small, padded chair, Todd flopping onto the bed.

"I think you know what this is all about," she began, then proceeded to outline what Jud had said to her, omitting that he had asked to buy her stock.

"Dammit, Anne, we told Jud weeks ago we wanted no part of this."

Troy sprang out of the chair and walked around the room impatiently. Todd merely grunted his agreement with Troy and massaged his temples.

"But I think he's right," Anne argued. "It is time for expansion, for moving ahead. If we stand still, we'll stagnate, become second rate."

"God, she sounds like Jud's echo," Todd told the ceiling disgustedly. Then, giving her a sharp look, rapped, "Whose side are you on, anyway?"

"Oh, Todd," Anne sighed wearily. "You sound like a little boy. I want what's best for the business, because in the long run it will be best for you two."

"Anne, listen." Sensing her growing impatience with them, Troy spoke soothingly. "We've talked to a lot of people in the mill this last week. Most of them agree with our opinion that we just can't handle a contract of this size. Regardless of what Jud thinks. The general consensus seems to be that if we take it on it will be the end of us."

"Honey," Todd began as soon as Troy had finished. "There is one thing you're forgetting. Jud is for number one, first, last, and always. I don't know what he is planning here, but you can bet he won't come out the loser. We will."

"But—"

"No buts," Troy stated firmly. "We're not going into this, Anne. That's final. And the sooner he's told the better. Maybe, if he's convinced he's not going to get his way, he'll get the hell out of here, go back to New York. He's in the library, why don't you go and brighten this dull day for him."

His last words were delivered in a malicious way and Anne found herself asking him the same question she'd asked Jud weeks before, only in reverse.

"Do you hate Jud, Troy?"

Oddly there was only minor differences in the answer.

"Hell, no," he replied mildly. "He is my brother. If you'll remember, both Todd and I had a pretty bad case of hero worship for him before he went away. The way he went, the fact that he never appeared again until Dad died, well, I resent it. And I just don't like him very much anymore."

"Ditto." This from Todd as he crawled off her bed.

After they left, Anne sat on the side of her bed,

128

brow puckered in thought. Could they be right about Jud? She didn't want to believe it, but, then, what she wanted had very little to do with it. She had heard the rumors that had run like wildfire from the mill to the offices. One claimed that this other company was really planning a takeover and that all the employees would lose their seniority. Another that Jud was deliberately taking on more than they could handle in order to run the company at a loss and thereby claim a tax write-off.

As always with scuttlebutt she had shaken her head and dismissed it. Now she had doubts and she didn't like it. She had realized from the beginning that Jud was dangerous, ruthless, and bitter. But would he ruin the company his father had worked all his life to build? She couldn't believe it. She wouldn't believe it. At least not without more proof. And she wasn't going to learn anything sitting here thinking in circles. Jumping to her feet, Anne went to her dresser, brushed her hair, straightened her gauze shirt and ran damp palms over her jean-clad hips. Giving one last nervous glance into the mirror, Anne grimaced, turned, and left the room.

When she reached the library, Anne hesitated; then, straightening her shoulders, she knocked on the door and pushed it open. Jud was speaking into a Dictaphone but he clicked it off as she entered.

"Good morning," he murmured, then went straight to the point. "Have you talked to Troy and Todd?"

"Yes." Anne sat down on the edge of the chair he nodded at before adding, "They were—ah—difficult."

"Tell me about it," Jud drawled.

Anne wet her lips and stared at him. It seemed he was going to be somewhat difficult himself.

"Jud, they absolutely refuse to consider it."

"You explained my reasoning?"

129

"Yes, of course. I—"

"Well?"

The tone of his voice warned her he was going to be very difficult.

"They've been discussing it with some of the mill employees this week and, well, it appears everyone is of the opinion that it can't be done."

Pale eyebrows shot up in a face turned cold and haughty.

"My dear Anne." The sarcastic note flicked along her nerves. "Company policy is not necessarily made on the workroom floor."

"Jud, they're afraid it's a takeover bid, or worse."

"Really?" he snapped. "And you?"

Anne was beginning to understand the feelings of a cornered animal.

"I don't know, I . . ."

She stopped and leaned back in her seat, for Jud stood up so violently she felt threatened.

"Come here."

Without taking his eyes from hers, he flipped open a folder on his desk. Before she could move, he was around the desk and in front of her, suppressed fury in his eyes.

"It's all in there," he indicated the folder. "Plans, proposed changes, approximate costs, minutes of the negotiations, everything to date."

He turned to the door as he added, "While you go over it, I'm going to hunt up some coffee. Do you want some?"

"Yes, please," she replied, then winced as the door slammed behind him.

It didn't take long. A few pages into the folder and Anne knew the twins and whomever they had talked to were wrong. She was still reading when Jud came

130

back into the room, a mug of coffee in each hand, but she really didn't have to see any more.

Jud handed her a mug, then propped himself on the edge of the desk, his eyes glittering with anger.

"Are you satisfied?"

"Yes."

Anne bent her head to stare into the creamy brew.

"And are you going to sell me your stock?"

Her head jerked up and she had to grasp her cup to keep from spilling the hot liquid.

"Jud, I can't. You know that."

"Can't has nothing to do with it." The purr was back in his voice and Anne decided she'd rather hear the anger.

"What you mean is, you won't."

"Jud, please, try to understand my position."

"I understand it perfectly. You're afraid that if you sell to me I'll force them out. You refuse to trust me, refuse to believe I have their interests as much on my mind as you do."

He paused and Anne began to feel prickly under his brooding stare. What could she say? She wanted to trust him. But he was right, she was afraid. Even loving him as much as she did hadn't changed that.

His soft voice intruded on her thoughts. "I have an alternative, Anne."

"An alternative? What possible alternative could there be?"

Her mind darted back and forth but, for the life of her, she couldn't come up with one.

His softly purred words went through her like an electric shock.

"Marry me."

131

CHAPTER

9

Marry me. Marry me. Marry me.

The words seemed to reverberate through her mind like the aftereffects of an explosion. Stunned, feeling as if she were caught in a vise that was slowly squeezing the air out of her body, Anne stared at him mutely, unable for several minutes to articulate even the smallest word. Had he gone mad or had she? He couldn't be serious. Or could he? The idea that he'd even consider giving up his freedom just to get control of the company was beyond her comprehension. When finally she managed to lossen her tension-taut vocal cords, her voice came in a strangled squeak.

"Marry you? How could that solve anything?"

"I would think the answer to that would be evident," he replied smoothly. "Actually the benefits would be twofold."

Her throat working spasmodically, Anne brought a measure of normalcy to her tone.

"I must be a little slow this morning, for I fail to see—"

"Anne," Jud chided gently, "get with it. If you marry me, you could support me in this, and possibly future deals, without actually giving up control of your stock. At the same time you'd still hold the

132

check rein the old man intended. Being my wife would in no way compel you to go along with anything I wanted to do. But, at the same time, as my wife I'd know that once given, your support would not be withdrawn."

"As you suspect it would be otherwise?" Anne asked sharply.

"Might be," he corrected. "You have one very weak spot, Anne, and that's your love for Troy and Todd. There would always be the outside chance they would get to you. I don't care to take that chance."

"But, but if I agree to be—" She couldn't even think the words—be your wife—let alone say them. "To go along with your idea, Troy and Todd will think—"

"Of course," he interrupted impatiently, "for a while. Until they finally realize I'm not out to rob them of their inheritance. They are Cammerons, and I don't think it will be too long before their basic intelligence overrides their resentment."

And then what, Anne thought dismally, the dissolution of a marriage made in expediency? Before she could voice her thoughts, Jud veered from Troy and Todd.

"I said the benefits would be twofold. The first, of course, would be to me, but the second would be solely yours."

An intriguing piece of bait thrown out casually, Anne bit at once.

"In what way?"

"You could save face by beating Andrew to the altar."

Beating Andrew to the . . . Anne's eyes went wide.

"Andrew is getting married?"

"Well-ll—" Jud drew the word out thoughtfully. "I

can't answer a definite yes on that. I do know he has made a proposal. I also know the lady is giving it serious consideration."

The idea of Andrew getting married didn't bother her in the least, but she was curious.

"What lady?"

The answer came fast, flat, and emotionless.

"Lorna."

Anne's eyes closed against the sudden pain in her chest. Change twofold to threefold, and number three is the real and most important one. How any woman could consider Andrew over Jud mystified Anne. But then, perhaps Jud had never made a proposal to Lorna. At least not of a legal nature. Anne didn't like the direction her thoughts were galloping in, but one in particular would not be denied. Lorna could not give Jud what he coveted the most. The control of the company he thought of as rightfully his. How much he coveted it hit Anne where she hurt the most. Not only was he willing to give up his freedom to get it. He was willing to give up the woman he loved as well.

"Well, Anne?" Jud prompted.

Anne kept her eyes tightly closed, her mind working furiously. Could she do it? Could she commit herself to a man so ruthless he'd cast aside the woman he loved to achieve his ambition? The answer came clear and simple. Yes. Only a few short weeks before she had begged him silently to name his price, had vowed she'd pay anything. Her feelings had not changed, except perhaps to grow stronger. Being his wife and not his love would not be easy to live with. But the eventuality of being separated from him completely was totally unbearable. So, right or wrong, she was still willing to pay the price.

"Anne?"

To Anne's distracted mind Jud's tone seemed to hold a note of anxious hesitation. Jud anxious? With a brief shake of her head, Anne dismissed the possibility. Lifting her lids, she looked steadily into Jud's hooded amber eyes.

"All right, Jud. I'll do whatever you say."

His breath was expelled slowly, indicating exactly how anxious he really had been. Well, of course he was, Anne mused unhappily. He had taken a shot at his own particular star, now he could relax, his shot had hit its target.

"Anne, I—" He hesitated, as if groping for words, then, becoming brisk, all business, he stated. "I want to do it as soon as possible. These people are getting edgy and I'm not going any further on this contract until I have my ring on your finger and your word on your compliance with my wishes. We'll set the wheels in motion tomorrow morning, but meanwhile, I think we'd better make an announcement to the family at the lunch table." He eyed her warily before adding, "Does that meet with your approval?"

Anne sighed in resignation. What did it matter? It was a business arrangement, wasn't it? To insist on the usual fuss and flutter would not only be farcical, it would be blatant hypocrisy.

"I've already said I'll do whatever you say, Jud." Anne paused, then added softly, "It really doesn't matter when or how, does it?"

In the action of leaning back to pick up the folder on his desk, Jud turned back to her sharply, his eyes glittering with an emotion totally unfathomable to Anne.

Certain she did not want to hear what he was about to say, Anne jumped to her feet and hurried to the door.

"If we have an announcement to make, I think I'd better freshen up and change."

She had just stepped into her room when he caught up with her and, giving her a gentle push, he followed her in and closed the door.

"Anne, we have got to discuss how we're going to handle this."

He strolled across the room and dropped lazily into the chair Troy had vacated such a short time before.

"If your mother and the twins get even a hint at the reason for this marriage, the silent rebellion they've been engaging in will turn into open warfare."

He ran his eyes over her speculatively, then asked dryly, "How good an actress are you?"

"Actress? I don't understand."

Raising his eyes, as if seeking assistance from above, he sighed heavily.

"Sweetheart, I think the remark you made earlier about being a little slow today was a gross understatement. I mean, darling,"—the darling was heavily emphasized—"that we are going to have to play to the gallery. Convince them we have suddenly fallen deeply, urgently in love. In other words, we have got to clean up our act. If we continue taking verbal potshots at each other they'll be on to the play in no time. Now, do you understand?"

"Oh, perfectly, darling." She added even more emphasis to the darling, but some of the impact was lost as her voice wobbled. "Curtain up, let the play begin."

His soft laugh attacked her nervous system and, feeling her suddenly weak legs would no longer support her, she sank onto the bed.

"You are one fantastic little girl, you know that, chicken?"

If his laughter had undermined her poise, the silky purr he used on her now threatened to destroy her completely. In one fluid movement he was on his feet and moving across the room to her. One long finger hooked her chin, lifted her head.

"As they said in practically every cowboy movie ever made"—his voice took on the twang of a heavy western drawl—"you'll do to ride the river with, pardner."

Dipping his head, he placed his mouth against hers and murmured, "A kiss in lieu of a contract, Anne." Then the pressure of his lips increased and his mouth, causing her heart to jump like a demented acrobat, drove out all reason and sanity.

"Yes, indeed," he whispered as he lifted his head after a few long moments. "You'll do very nicely. Now, I'll let you get changed, as Margaret and Melly are back from church and ready for lunch."

He had reached the door before Anne had gathered her wits enough to ask haltingly, "Jud, about this marriage. Will it be . . . I mean will you want—" She faltered, searching for words.

"A normal sexual relationship?" he supplied softly.

Anne swallowed hard, then nodded. His face gave away nothing of what he felt, his eyes remained steady on hers.

"Yes."

A final, no-questions-asked yes.

"But, I never—" Anne bit down on her lip. "I mean, I don't know if I can. I—"

"Oh, you can," he countered. "The way you respond to my kisses convinces me of that." He studied the pink stain spreading across her cheeks a moment, then added gently, "But don't worry, honey. I'm a patient man, and I'll be very careful not to rush or frighten you."

After a quick shower Anne slipped into a light, cotton dress, applied a touch of color to lids, cheeks, and lips, and was finishing her hairdo when her door opened. Jud stood in the hall freshly showered and shaved, looking far too attractive in dark brown slacks and antique gold shirt.

"Are you ready to go down?" he asked quietly. "I think it would be best to confront them together and get it over with."

Nervous, and trying hard not to show it, Anne licked her dry lips.

"Yes, I'm ready."

She left the room and walked beside him down the hall to the top of the stairs, where she paused, throwing him a quick glance.

"Do you want me to tell them or will you?"

"I think I'd better." He shot her a brief, devastating grin. "Your voice is none too steady." He started down the stairs, his hand grasping hers. "Don't give yourself away, Anne," he cautioned. "Or all hell will break loose. Just follow my lead and we'll be home free."

As they entered the dining room, Jud's hand released Anne's and slid protectively around her waist.

The action did not go unnoticed. Anne saw the surprise that filled her mother's eyes, the question that narrowed both Troy's and Todd's. Only Melly seemed unaware of the sudden tension in the room.

"About time you two showed up," Melly scolded lightly. "I'm famished. For some strange reason a long, uninspired sermon always makes me hungry. Now we can eat."

"In a moment." Jud's quiet, serious tone sent his aunt's eyebrows up. Anne felt his hand tighten at her waist, then he said calmly, "Anne and I are going to be married."

He could not have achieved a better effect if he had dropped a snake onto the table. Melly looked stunned, Todd and Troy jumped out of their chairs, and Margaret gave a small disbelieving shriek.

"You are what?"

"Getting married."

Jud's unruffled reply seemed to incite rather than calm them.

"But you can't," Margaret gasped.

"Can't?" One pale eyebrow arched arrogantly. "I assure you we can."

"But, Jud," her mother moaned. "Anne is your stepsister."

"Step being the operative word," he retorted. "It has no bearing at all."

"Now who's playing games, Jud?" Troy's voice was nasty. "And what's the name of this one? Force the twins into line?"

Todd's eyes, their color cloudy with an equal mixture of anger and hurt, fastened on Anne's.

"Or should we substitute the word blackmail for games? I might have expected something like this from him, Anne. But not you. Never you."

Anne paled. Jud's face went rigid and Margaret cried, "Todd!"

During the exchange Melly's head had swiveled from one to the other, her confusion mirrored on her face. Her glance settling on Jud, she sighed.

"I don't understand. What is the problem, Jud? Personally I'm delighted."

Jud's face softened, and he smiled gently at his aunt.

"Thank you, Mel. Don't be alarmed. There is no problem here I can't handle."

"Big man," Troy spat. "You're not forcing me into anything. You'd sell your soul to get your own way down at the mill, wouldn't you? Well, you can go to hell." His furious glance pierced Anne, and she gasped as he added, "And you can go with him."

Anne felt Jud go stiff beside her, felt the sharp pain as his fingers dug spasmodically into her waist. He frightened her. Everything about him frightened her, from his contempt-filled, cold eyes, to the still, coiled menace that emanated from every inch of him. Finally his chillingly soft purr broke the silence that had gripped the room.

"I don't have to force you into anything, Troy. You'll do as you're told." His voice went softer still, causing a shiver to tingle along Anne's arms. "And if you ever speak to your sister like that again, I will take the hide off your back. Strip by slow strip. Now make your apology."

Again the room was smothered in silence and Anne's fingers curled into her damp palms. When she felt Jud move in Troy's direction, she moaned softly.

"Troy, please."

Troy's eyes, wary and fear-filled, shifted to Anne's pale face and with a soft sigh of defeat he murmured, "I'm sorry, Anne."

"Jud?"

Although her voice was steady, Melly's eyes betrayed her unease.

"It's all right, Mel."

The change in him was almost unbelievable. Relaxed and easy, he laughed lazily, then drawled, "As a wedding gift to Anne, I'll let him live—this week."

The tension was broken. Melly's eyes laughed back at him.

"You're a devil, you know that?" she chided teasingly. "How dull my life would be without you." Her eyes lit with a mischief of their own. "Do you think

140

you could stop playing El Macho long enough to give me some lunch?"

Jud threw back his head and laughed, the warm sound melting the ice Anne seemed to be enclosed in. Lunch was served and, although Troy and Todd remained resentfully quiet, Margaret finally gave in and joined the conversation to back up Jud's invitation to Melly to stay over for the ceremony.

"I wouldn't miss your wedding, Jud—" Melly's eyes shifted to the twins "—any more than I'd miss Troy and Todd when they decide to take the plunge. Of course I'll have to call home but, as Frank's been doing so well, I'm sure it will be all right. Your Uncle Frank will be disappointed he can't be here as well."

The meal proceeded at a leisurely pace, Margaret, with Melly's prodding, getting into the swing of the sparse arrangements when she suggested, hopefully, that Anne and Jud wait, if only long enough for her to plan a proper, as she put it, wedding, but Jud shook his head uttering a decided "No."

Neck muscles tight with tension, pain beginning to throb at her temples, Anne thought the meal would never end. When finally they left the table, Anne sighed in relief and excused herself.

"I have a slight headache," she murmured when Jud asked quietly if something was wrong. "It must be the excitement."

Wanting to run, forcing herself to walk, she hurried up the stairs and into her room. She was standing at the window, staring at the black, angry-looking clouds, when the sound of her door being opened was muffled by a loud nerve-jarring crack of lightning that rent the sky directly overhead.

Anne gasped, startled by the sudden violence of nature, then gasped again when large, masculine hands came down onto her shoulders.

"Getting cold feet, Anne?"

Jud's voice was low and, coming as it did with the sudden downpour of rain, Anne could not suppress a shudder or the tight note in her voice.

"No."

"Good, because I'm not about to let you back out."

His cool breath ruffled across the top of her head, his soft tone ruffled across her heart. Drawing a deep breath, steeling herself against the craziness of her body's response to his nearness, she replied steadily.

"The thought of backing out hadn't occurred to me."

"No?"

His fingers loosened and he moved closer until, his forearms resting lightly on her shoulders, his body was only a tingling whisper away from hers.

"Then why did you come tearing up here the minute lunch was over?"

"I really do have a headache, and I was upset." She hesitated, then added sadly, "I knew Todd and Troy wouldn't like the idea of us getting married, but I didn't expect—" She broke off, a sigh replacing the rest of the words.

His arms came toward her, crossed at the base of her neck, drawing her closer still to his body. Bending his head until it was lying beside hers, he said softly, "They'll get over it, Annie. You've all spoiled them, but I don't believe they're vindictive. They'll come around."

"I hope so, Jud." A small sob caught in her throat as she added, "It will all be so pointless if they don't."

At her words he went taut, his arms tightening their hold.

"Anne!"

At that moment another loud crack of lightning knifed the sky, followed by a window-rattling roll of thunder. Cringing back against him, she closed her eyes with a shudder. His teasing laughter tickled her earlobe.

"Surely you're not afraid of storms, little girl?"

"No, of course not." Her answer was quick and emphatic. "It was just so close, it startled me. And I wish you wouldn't call me little girl."

"Why not?" he murmured against her ear. "You are little and you sure as hell are a girl."

His hands moved caressingly over her shoulders, down her arms, causing a chill to feather her spine, fire to lick her blood.

"Soft too." His lips moved maddeningly down her neck, and she gasped when his tongue slid lightly along the curve of her shoulder. "Taste good, too. No doubt about it. You are definitely a girl."

The earlier unpleasantness, the tension, her headache, all combined with a sudden onslaught of desire that left her trembling and teary. Shaken by the depth of her own hunger for him, she went stiff.

"Jud, you must stop this."

"Why must I stop?"

His hand moved from her arm, fingers bringing devastation as they slid across her collarbone, down the V of her dress.

"I don't want to stop, Anne, I want you and I think you want me too."

His confidence, his obvious experience against her total inexperience, made her wary. And with her caution came the bitter thought, *He's getting everything he wants so easily that now he thinks he can have me easily as well*. The very idea that he could think of her as easy quenched the fire in her veins. Bringing her hands up to grasp his arms, she pulled them apart, stepped away from him.

"You're mistaken, Jud," she said flatly, then barbed

coldly as he moved toward her. "You're using me to get what you want in the firm. I won't let you use me physically as well."

Incredulity, followed by blazing anger, narrowed his eyes. In an oddly strained hoarse tone, he growled, "Use you? That isn't what I would have said, but never mind."

He turned abruptly and walked to the door, then with his hand on the knob he turned back and said coldly, "Don't worry, Anne. I won't bother you with my attentions again. And I hope you freeze in your bed."

The soft click of the door closing behind him sent a shaft of pure misery through Anne. Anyone coming along the hall and hearing his last words may have looked out of the window and been puzzled, for it was June—stormy, warm, and sticky. But Anne knew what he meant and she was very much afraid that his hope would be realized.

The following week was full of uncertainty and un-happiness for Anne. At the breakfast table Monday, Jud stated calmly that Anne was not to go into the office that week. Anne and Jud were alone in the dining room, as Margaret and Melly were not yet up and Troy and Todd had already left the house, presumably choosing to go without breakfast rather than sit at the table with Jud and Anne.

"Not go in?" Anne felt the first stirrings of uncertainty. "But why?"

"Anne," Jud sighed patiently, "I told you I want to do this as fast as possible and one assumes that every girl has things to do the week before her wedding."

"But this isn't a normal wedding," Anne insisted rashly. "And I'm not the usual blushing bride."

Jud's eyes and tone went hard. "I know that. But no one else does, do they? You agreed yesterday to play this to the hilt. Have you changed your mind since then?"

Her uncertainty deepened at the sharp edge to his voice and with surprise she realized he was very, very angry. But why? Did his anger stem from frustration at being rejected the night before? Not wanting to even think about that, Anne answered quickly.

"No, I haven't, but I don't see what that has to do with—"

Her words faltered when he pushed his chair back angrily and stood up. Looking down at her coldly, he seemed to tower over her and unconsciously Anne shrank back against her chair. His eyes and face mirrored his scorn and he grated, "Relax, I'm not going to touch you, and I have no time to stay here arguing with you, either. I have a lot to do this week if I'm going to be out of the office next week."

"Out of the office," she repeated in astonishment. "But why?"

Apparently his patience had reached the end of its tether.

"If you can refrain from interrupting," he snapped, "I will explain why."

Speechless for the moment, Anne nodded mutely.

"I would like to have the ceremony Sunday." He paused, then added sarcastically, "If that meets with your approval?"

Again the mute nod.

"Very well. I would also like to leave for New York immediately after the ceremony, as I have several appointments there next week I can't miss. Are you with me so far?"

Uncertainty was being nudged aside by his condescending tone, and Anne hissed, "Yes."

"Good," he hissed back. "I want you to meet me for lunch at one at the Elegant Spoon. While we eat

145

I'll outline the arrangements I've made to that point. All right?"

Anne nodded angrily.

"Okay. Now, if you'll excuse me," he jibed nastily, "I have work to do."

He strode from the room and Anne sat perfectly still for several minutes, her hands clenched into tight fists. Who in the hell did he think he was? she fumed. The memory of his cool voice taunted, *"The Boss."*

Her anger still a fierce glow inside, Anne met Jud at the restaurant. The anger was soon coupled with amazement as, forcing food down her throat, she heard him tick off the arrangements he'd made during the morning. Everything was taken care of, he told her smoothly, ignoring the warning flash in her eyes, from their stop directly after lunch at the license bureau, to a later one with a doctor for the blood test, on through the name of the district justice who would perform the ceremony and the time of their flight to New York afterward.

Anne's mind latched onto the last of his plans.

"I'm to go with you to New York?"

Jud opened his mouth, then closed it again with a snap, glancing around the well-filled room as if suddenly aware of where he was. White lines of anger tinting his lips, he drew a long, deliberate breath through nostrils flaring in fury.

"Of course you're to go with me, you fool. By then you will be my wife."

Reaching across the table he grasped her hand painfully and, although his voice was low, none of its fierceness was lost.

"My God, girl, how would it look if I left you alone on our wedding night? Will you start thinking, please?"

146

His attitude toward her the rest of that afternoon was one of cool, withdrawn politeness. In growing wonder Anne observed the deference Jud was accorded wherever they went and the speed with which his smallest request was carried out. She had had no idea he had so many friends, and in such high places. It became increasingly obvious to her that as far as Jud was concerned, when he set a ball in motion, that object damned well better roll, and smoothly. For herself Anne was beginning to feel as if it were rolling over her, somewhat in the manner of an avalanche.

By the time Anne slid into bed that night, the bemusement and wonder that had kept her quiet and docile all afternoon began to burn off, leaving in its wake a residue of cold resentment.

Other than the actual day of their marriage, she had not been consulted at all about the other arrangements, she thought furiously. And if she was not to go to the office, exactly what was she to do with the rest of the week? Twiddle her thumbs like a good little girl? *Bump him,* she decided scathingly. She damned well would go to the office, and just let him try and send her home again. The decision made, Anne rolled over and went to sleep.

Her rest deep and undisturbed for once by nightmares, Anne woke refreshed and prepared to face any obstacle the day might bring, including Judson Cammeron.

In a mood of defiance she abstained from joining Jud at the breakfast table, waited at her bedroom window until she saw him back the El Dorado out of the garage, then, avoiding her mother and Melly, slipped out of the house and drove to the mill—in her own car.

She had no sooner closed her bottom desk drawer

when Jud's voice barked from the connecting room, "Anne, come in here."

Swallowing back the sudden brackish taste of fear that rose in her throat, Anne squared her shoulders, set her chin at an obstinate angle, and walked slowly into his office.

Leaning back lazily in his swivel chair, his hands toying with a pen, he looked deceptively relaxed and pleasant.

"I thought we'd agreed you would not come in this week." His voice matched his demeanor in deception.

"I don't remember agreeing to anything of the kind," she replied with forced mildness. "You said you have a lot to do this week; well, so have I. And it's not going to get done if I sit at home cooling my heels all week."

He moved forward with a snap and, casting aside all pretense, he let his annoyance show by flinging his pen onto the desk.

"Have you no sense of self-preservation at all? Why the hell do you even want to be here this week? Do you have masochistic tendencies?"

Taken aback by the force and harshness of his attack, Anne stepped back in alarm.

"I—I don't understand?"

"Don't you, really?" he sneered. "Tell me you haven't heard the rumors."

Jud stared at Anne intently a few seconds, then, apparently deciding she was truly ignorant as to what he was talking about, he walked around his desk to her. His face inches from hers, he raised his brows exaggeratedly.

"Where have you been the last few weeks, permanently out to lunch? How did you manage to miss the stupid female, and male, twitters emanating from the outer offices?"

His exasperation with her was a tangibly felt presence reaching out to figuratively shake her. Feeling stifled by that presence, she snapped, "Do you think you could leave off with the insults and tell me what these rumors were?"

"Of a very basic nature," he bit back. "Having to do with the convenience of us living in the same house, if you get my drift?"

Anne's eyes flew wide with shock.

"But that's ridiculous!"

"How well I know it," he drawled sarcastically. "But not unexpected from a certain type of malicious mind."

Stunned beyond speech, Anne just stared at him biting her lip savagely. He watched her, hard-faced, for some time, then, with a sigh that sounded like one of defeat, he said softly, "Anne, you know as well as I do that our sudden decision to marry will run like wildfire through this place. And that the general consensus will be that you are pregnant. By asking you to stay away this week I was simply trying to spare you the embarrassment of listening to their stupid gossip. Now, will you go home?"

"No."

Unable to withstand the renewed flare of anger in his eyes, Anne lowered her own, studying the carpet as if it were the most fascinating thing she'd ever seen.

"Dammit, Anne, why must you be so stubborn?"

Grasping her arms, he gave her a little shake, jerking her head up in the process. Shrugging herself free of his hands, she moved away from him.

"Probably because I grew up surrounded by Cammerons."

He rewarded her with a quick grin and made bold by his softened expression, she went on, "I'm not all

149

that fragile, Jud. If I overhear the gossip, I'll dismiss it, as I've done with all the gossip I've heard here."

With a shrug that said "Do as you please," he gave in with a brusque, "Okay, if you're determined to stay, let's get to work."

Being in the office helped her get through the week, but even so, as Sunday loomed ever closer, her stomach proceeded to tie itself into tiny little knots.

CHAPTER

10

It was over. She was his wife!

The enormity of the step she'd taken didn't hit Anne until she was strapped into her seat and the plane was making its takeoff run. What in the world was she doing here? she asked herself a little wildly. Had she gone totally and completely crazy? For one very small moment panic clutched at her throat and she had to fight the urge to flip open her seat belt and run. Run where? The plane was airborne and in less than an hour they'd be landing in Newark.

Reason swiftly reasserted itself, but even so, Anne sat, body pressed against the cushioned padding, hands gripping the arms of her seat.

"Does flying frighten you?"

Caught up in her own thoughts, the sound of Jud's voice strongly tinged with concern startled Anne so much that she jumped.

"For heaven's sake, Anne, relax." Jud's hand covered hers, pried her fingers loose, and laced his long ones through hers before adding, "Flying's safer than driving today."

"I know that."

Anne moistened dry lips, casting about in her mind for a plausible excuse for her tension, when she

151

caught a flash of gold out of the corner of her eyes. Although the morning had dawned bright and sunny, by lunchtime the brightness had turned a brassy color and the air had grown oppressive; and by the time they had left for the airport black clouds were building in the west, long fingers of lightning poking through them. Anne grasped at the weather for an excuse.

"Generally I love flying," she said slowly, darting a quick glance at the small window. "But not when there's a storm brewing. I don't like taking off and landing when there's lightning about."

Jud laughed softly, a gentle, reassuring laugh that rippled along Anne's tension-tight nerve ends.

"We'll be down before you know it," he soothed, then, his fingers tightening, he leaned closer to her and murmured, "Hang on to me, honey, and everything will be all right."

In confusion Anne lowered her eyes. Had there been a double meaning to his words? That amber gaze had been so intent, as if trying to tell her something. But what? You're being fanciful, she chided herself scathingly, her eyes fastened on her small hand, held so firmly and securely in his much larger one. *He is merely trying to keep me calm,* she reasoned dismally, *insuring himself against the embarrassment of a hysterical woman.*

The plane landed smoothly and, in an amazingly short time, their valises had been collected and Anne found herself being ushered into the back of the hired limo that was waiting for them. Jud settled himself on the seat beside her, recaptured her hand, then asked softly, "Better now?"

Idly his fingers played with the thin gold band on her finger, sending tiny shivers up her arm. In an effort to cover the small sound her catching breath made, Anne laughed shakily and nodded an answer.

"Good," Jud murmured lazily, then cocked an eyebrow at her. "Would you like to stop for dinner on the way or do you want to go straight home?"

Home? The word doubled her shivers, pushed them up and over her shoulders, down into her stomach.

"I—I think we'd better go straight h— to the apartment," she finally got past the lump in her throat, "if we don't want to get caught in the deluge," she added, turning to look out the window at the steadily lowering black clouds.

"You may be right," he agreed in an unconcerned tone. "Although, at the rate of speed this traffic's moving, we may be caught in it anyway."

They just made it. For no more than five minutes after reaching the apartment the greenish-black sky seemed to be torn apart by the fury of the storm.

Jud's apartment was in a good neighborhood, large, and obviously expensive. Consisting of two bedrooms, one bath, a small, fully equipped kitchen, and a large living room, it had the added advantage of several large windows which afforded at least a glimpse of Central Park.

Nervous to the point of feeling sick, Anne moved silently beside Jud as he gave her the grand tour ending in the kitchen and nearly jumped when his soft voice broke the quiet.

"Are you hungry? The fridge has been stocked and I'm sure that between the two of us we could rustle up something edible."

"I—I'm not too hungry," she hedged, the very thought of food causing her stomach to jump.

He was standing indolently, one hip propped

against the countertop and the sardonic expression he wore prompted her to add quickly, "I could drink some coffee, though." Then hesitantly, "Are you hungry?"

"Actually I'm famished," he drawled. "But I can make do with a sandwich. I have before."

A small twinge of guilt put a touch of color to her pale cheeks. He was hungry and she had turned down his offer to stop. The least she could do was make him something hot to eat, she told herself contritely. Besides which, it was a way of filling in some of the hours that stretched between now and bedtime.

"A sandwich isn't enough, I'll cook something." Jud's look of mild surprise prompted her to add. "Although I'm no Cordon Bleu chef, I can get a meal together."

"I didn't suggest you couldn't," he retorted softly. His face thoughtful, he studied her a moment. "There's no hurry. I'll get some steaks out of the freezer to thaw. You look washed out, why don't you go have a shower and rest for an hour or so?"

"Rest?" Anne was almost afraid to ask. "Where?"

His soft sigh told her of his impatience as clearly as hard words would have.

"I put your suitcase in the spare bedroom, Anne." Long fingers raked through that fantastic gold hair. "Go. Get some rest. It's been a long day." His hand slid to the back of his neck, massaging slowly as he flexed suddenly bunched-up shoulder muscles. "Hell, it's been one long week. Go on," he urged. "You have a shower and a nap. I'll have a shower and a drink. On second thought, maybe I'll have several drinks."

"On an empty stomach, Jud?"

He had turned to stare out the small window above the sink, but on her hesitant question he whirled around, his face hard, his eyes mocking.

154

"Good God! Did I acquire a wife or a mother this afternoon?"

Stepping back at his harsh tone, Anne could actually feel her face pale. Wide eyed, hurt, she stammered, "I—I'm—sorry. I—"

"Yes, Anne," he interrupted wearily. "So am I. Don't concern yourself, I'll have some pretzels with the booze." Giving his shoulders another sharp jerk, he ordered, "Get out of here, and don't come back for at least"—he glanced at his watch "—an hour and a half."

"Jud."

"Beat it. You may have the bathroom for exactly twenty minutes. If you're not out of the shower by then I'll join you in it."

Anne spun around and fled, his derisive laughter chasing her through the living room.

Fourteen minutes later Anne stepped out of the bathroom feeling cool and refreshed, if still somewhat shaky. In the few steps required to reach her room she had neither sight nor sound of Jud. With a sigh of relief she slipped inside the room, closing the door quietly.

The room, though not as large as Jud's, was of adequate size, furnished with a high-glossed pine suite. The walls were covered by a rough-textured, burlap-weave paper, the woodwork painted a satiny white. Draperies, bedspread, and carpet were all in a matching burnt orange that lent color to the otherwise bland decor. This room, Anne decided, was at once comfortable and impersonal. A fact that suited her mood.

Dropping onto the bed, Anne turned her head to the window, studying the zigzag pattern of the draperies as she relived the earlier part of the day with a vague feeling of unreality.

She had wakened that morning encased in a deadly calm which, by mid-afternoon, had deepened into a cold numbness. Both her mother and Melly had flittered around the house all day, seemingly very busy. For the life of her, Anne could not imagine what kept them so occupied. Except for a few minutes at lunchtime, Anne did not see much of Jud and she didn't catch hide nor hair of the twins until they tore into the house an hour before it was time to leave.

Someone had gotten to them. Either her mother or Melly or both. Anne suspected that Troy and Todd had been subjected to lectures from both their mother and their aunt. In any case their attitude, at least toward Anne, had softened. They accorded Jud a very thin civility, which, if his own attitude was anything to go by, did not bother him at all. Most surprising was that they had agreed to stand up as witnesses for Jud. Melly, flushed and delighted at being asked, would do the honors for Anne.

Even dressing for her own wedding had very little effect on Anne. She went through the motions slowly and carefully, standing back automatically to observe the finished product. The dress she wore, a simple summer shift in oyster white raw silk, was not new. Anne had bought the dress the previous summer, along with her shoes and bag in bronze patent leather. As she ran a practiced eye over her small form, Anne decided the overall impression was definitely blah. But then that was exactly how she felt, so, with a light shrug of her shoulders, she silently declared herself ready.

The actual ceremony could not have taken more then eight minutes but, even though she was still in a numb, unfeeling cocoon, two things filtered through and registered with Anne. First, the words of the service were the traditional ones, including love, honor, and obey. Second, the district justice, a slim attractive woman in her early forties, read them with such solemnity and force, Anne was left in little doubt as to how serious the woman considered the act of marriage.

Her calm had remained unshaken during the cheek-kissing and fervent wishes of happiness she received from her mother and Melly as they paused a few moments beside the car outside the district justice's office. Not even the last-minute surrender of Troy and Todd, given in the form of a fierce hug from each in turn and the softly muttered "I pray you'll be happy, Anne" from Troy, hadn't really touched her. It was not until she was actually on the plane that the full realization of it all struck her like a physical blow.

Now, some three hours later, she lay in an unfamiliar bed in the guest room of Jud's apartment and the shock had worn off, leaving in its stead the sick cry—what have I done?

Exactly at the time stipulated, Anne, in brown slacks and white gauze shirt, went into the kitchen. One step inside the archway that separated the kitchen from the living room she stopped, a bubble of disbelieving laughter catching at her throat, a forlorn pain catching at her heart.

Jud stood back to her at the countertop, chopping vegetables for a salad, his just-shampooed hair glint ing like a newly minted gold coin, and he was dressed, amazingly, in brown brushed denim jeans and white gauze shirt. On hearing her enter, he turned, and Anne could see a tiny piece of glittering gold chain at the unbuttoned neck of his shirt.

"The steaks have thawed enough to remove the wrapping and I've opened a bottle—" Having turned fully around, he stopped, eyes narrowing as they went

157

slowly over her. Then, with what looked like a bitter smile tugging at the corners of his mouth and what sounded like a muttered "unreal," he turned back to his task, continuing, "I've opened a bottle of Cabernet to let breathe awhile. Did you rest at all?"

"Yes," Anne lied calmly. "What can I do to help?"

"Put the steaks under the broiler, set the table, and start a pot of coffee, in that order." He returned with equal calm.

As she set the glass-topped, circular table, Anne felt positive she would not be able to eat. But one piece of the tender Delmonico and several sips of Cabernet seemed to revive her appetite and she not only finished all her steak and salad, she managed a small dish of fresh strawberries as well.

Conversation during the meal and the cleaning up was practically nil and Anne preceded Jud into the living room with trepidation when it was finally over.

Whatever would they talk about? Anne asked herself, warily eying the dark-brown, velvet-covered pit grouping that took up almost three-fourths of the room. Choosing the smallest of the two single chairs in the room, she slipped off her sandals and curled herself on it, sighing in relief as Jud strolled to the stereo unit and began flipping through a large stack of albums.

The music Jud chose did not have the calming effect Anne had hoped for. In fact the husky quality of Neil Diamond's voice combined with lyrics that too often touched a raw nerve increased her tension.

The second hand had chased itself some ninety times around the face of the clock, and Anne was beginning to fidget, when the arm lifted off the last record on the stereo. The sudden silence in the room was short-lived, for Jud's soft but harsh voice cracked it.

"For God's sake, Anne, go to bed."

Somewhat fearfully Anne lifted surprised eyes to him. He was sitting in the exact center of the pit, legs stretched out, head back, and Anne could not remember ever seeing him look quite so tired. His voice matched his expression in weariness.

"You sit there looking as if you'll jump out of your skin at the slightest move from me." He paused, his mouth twisting in mockery. "I assure you you'll be perfectly safe if you go to bed. Pouncing on unwilling women has never been my thing."

The bitterness and disgust that overlay his tone on his last words brought her to her feet in self-defense.

"Jud, I didn't mean to—"

"Get out of here, Anne," he sighed in exasperation. "Just shut up and go to bed."

He closed his eyes and Anne had the feeling that not only had he closed out the sight of her, but her entire existence as well. Cheeks pink, she retreated without another word.

A light tapping roused Anne and, coming awake quickly, she glanced around the room in confusion before realizing where she was. The last thing she remembered, after sliding between the sheets, was that she probably wouldn't sleep and now the room was bright with sunlight.

The tap sounded again, then the door was pushed open and Jud took one step into the room, looking brisk and all business in a fawn-colored, vested suit, crisp white shirt, and dark brown tie. His tone matched his appearance in briskness.

"Good morning. Sorry to wake you, but I'm ready to leave for the office and as I hate leaving notes, I thought I'd better warn you about Mrs. Doyle before she arrived and startled you. Mrs. Doyle comes in twice a week to clean the place and she's a regular whirlwind. If you don't stay out of her way she's liable to dust you along with the furniture so I'd advise you to vacate the premises. Do a little shopping. I've left you some money, it's on the kitchen count—"

"I don't need your mon—" Anne interrupted, only to be cut off herself.

"I don't have time to argue, Anne," he snapped, glancing pointedly at his watch. "I have an appointment in less than an hour. There's fresh coffee and muffins warming in the oven if you're hungry. I don't know what time I'll get home, probably not before six thirty, so don't bother about dinner, we'll go out somewhere. Take the money."

He was gone and Anne sat staring at the empty doorway, angry words of refusal dying on her lips. Gritting her teeth, she sat fuming several minutes, then a thought struck her, propelling her out of the bed with a muttered oath. This Mrs. Doyle would be coming to clean the rooms, including the bedrooms. Damned if she'd allow the woman to see the true status of their marriage.

Causing something of a small whirlwind of her own, Anne tidied and dusted her bedroom then moved on to Jud's, performing the same tasks there, while studiously not looking too closely at his personal things. Showered and dressed to go out, Anne was sitting at the table with her first cup of coffee when Mrs. Doyle arrived.

"You must be Mrs. Cammeron," the small, round woman began in a bland manner.

"Yes, but how—" Anne started, only to be cut off with an airy wave of a small, pudgy hand.

"Mr. Cammeron called me at home. Asked me not to disturb you if you'd gone back to sleep." Then she tacked on, "Oh, yes, congratulations. I hope you'll be very happy."

"Thank you," Anne murmured, amusement tugging at her lips. "Would you like a cup of coffee?"

"No, thank you. I have two other places to get to today, so I'd better get started."

She turned to the closet for the cleaning utensils and Anne, going to the sink to rinse her cup, said quickly. "Well, I've saved you some time, I did the bedroom, so all you have are the kitchen, living room, and bath." At the look of alarm that crossed the other woman's face, she added, "There will be no difference in your salary. I—I guess I just wanted to play at housewife a little." Although Anne considered her last words an inspiration, she nonetheless had to force them through her teeth. And with the strange look Mrs. Doyle gave her, she fled with a short, "I'm going shopping. Nice meeting you."

Feeling like a complete idiot, she left the apartment almost at a run, not slowing down until she was several blocks away.

For an hour Anne strolled listlessly through the shops, barely seeing the merchandise displayed, feeling none of the enthusiasm her previous shopping trips to New York had generated. Finally giving up, she walked for some time before coming to a stop before a movie theater. On the spur of the moment Anne bought a ticket and slipped inside to lose herself for several hours in the dimmed theater and the twisting, involved plot of a foreign film.

Anne was curled into one corner of the pit leafing through a magazine when Jud came in just before seven. He looked tired and short-tempered, his eyebrows inching up as he ran his flat amber gaze over her jeans and pullover, making her so nervous she stumbled over her explanation.

"The s-salad's tossed and—and there's a casserole in the oven."

"That wasn't necessary, we could have eaten out."

He crossed the living room, shrugging out of his jacket as he spoke, but although his tone was indifferent, Anne had the distinct impression he was relieved at not having to go out again.

It was not until they were back in the living room, dinner finished, this time listening to the upbeat sound of Chuck Mangione, that Jud threw out casually, "We'll go out tomorrow night, Anne. Maybe after dinner we'll take in that Swedish film everyone's talking about. They say it's very good."

"It is."

Anne sat biting her lips as he slowly straightened, the unasked question plain on his face.

"I—I didn't feel like shopping today," Anne spoke hurriedly. "So I went to a movie. I'm sorry, Jud."

He stared at her a long time, his expression strange, almost hurt, and Anne had to force herself to sit still and not squirm. Finally, when Anne thought she'd scream if he didn't say something, he said quietly, "Doesn't matter."

They stayed in New York until Friday, and Jud did not suggest going out again, either to the theater or dinner. In fact he didn't come home for dinner, saying the same thing to her each morning before he left. "Don't wait for me for dinner. I'll grab something somewhere close to the office. I have no idea what time I'll be home. Enjoy your day."

Enjoy your day. Anne raged silently. How does one go about enjoying anything when they're torn apart with uncertainty and—yes—jealousy. Was he really working? Surely not until after ten every night. If he's not working, where is he? Elementary, dummy—Lorna's place.

In an attempt to keep these, and other even more self-defeating thoughts at bay, Anne filled the hours of the day with sight-seeing and shopping, mostly on foot. At night she roamed the apartment, tired but unable to sleep or even sit for longer than a few minutes at a time. She made several surprising discoveries however. Apparently she and Jud shared more than their interest in his father's company. She found most of her favorite authors in his large collection of both hardcover and paperback books. She found they had like taste in popular as well as classical music as, by Thursday night, she had listened to almost every one of his records. And she loved the apartment. He had obviously decorated it himself, for everything about it seemed to whisper his name. Given free rein, Anne knew she'd have made very few, if any, changes. With so many things in common, why couldn't they be together for longer than thirty minutes without fighting? No answer presented itself to her silent question.

Anne boarded the plane for home Friday afternoon with mixed emotions. Relief at giving up her solitary existence in the apartment vied with unease at how Jud planned to carry off their mock marriage surrounded by family. She needn't have worried. As usual Jud had overlooked nothing.

"I've had a few changes made at the house while we've been away. I hope they meet with your approval."

Anne felt a flash of irritation at his bland, indifferent tone. As the changes were already made, did it make any difference if she didn't approve? In an effort to keep her voice calm, she pushed her question through stiff lips.

"Changes? What changes?"

He shot her a sharp glance, studying her tightly drawn features slowly before answering.

"Nothing earth-shattering, so take that trapped look off your face."

"What changes?" Anne hissed.

"I've had your things moved to the guest room on the other side of my bathroom."

Jud's room and the one her mother and his father had shared were the only bedrooms with private baths. Anne and her brothers had used the central bathroom that was entered from the hall. Unable to see the reason for the move, Anne said sharply, "Why?"

"Why do you think?" he snapped. Then he sighed and added softly, "I've also had a doorway cut into the wall between the guest room and the bathroom. Are you beginning to get the picture?"

"Perfectly. Will there be a lock on that door?"

His lips twisted scornfully. "You don't pull your punches, do you, Anne?"

For a moment his eyes glittered with anger, then with a shrug of indifference, he turned away from her, his tone bored.

"Yes, Anne, there will be a lock."

CHAPTER

11

The arrangement worked better than Anne would have suspected, even though she had bad moments, like entering the bathroom when the mirror was still cloudy from his shower steam and the air redolent with his cologne. At those times she was struck by a wave of longing so intense it took every ounce of willpower she possessed to keep from stepping through the door into his room.

Spring slipped into summer and Jud's plans for the company slipped into high gear. The much opposed contract was signed and the entire place was a beehive of activity and confusion. Jud moved through it all like the only sane man in a madhouse. He made a point of keeping Anne apprised of every move before it was made and for that she was grateful, for otherwise she'd have been as certain as practically everyone else that they would fail.

By mid-September Anne could see positive results emerging from what had looked like hopeless chaos. And as Jud's prediction that they could do it was proven correct, the attitude of the employees slowly changed from pessimistic to positive and supportive.

Anne had never worked so hard in her life. The amount of work Jud relegated to her as his assistant was enormous. No longer could she allow herself the luxury of going out for lunch, she simply could not spare the time. Instead she swallowed massive amounts of coffee and much smaller amounts of sandwiches at her desk, and not only at lunchtime but quite often at dinnertime as well.

She lost weight and, through the sunniest, hottest summer she could remember, acquired a decidedly unbecoming pallor. Her mother was vocal with concern, and when it became evident that Anne was not listening, she switched her complaints to Jud. Within days Anne's work load was cut considerably and she could feel Jud's brooding glance at regular intervals. His close observance of her had the opposite effect of what her mother had intended. Anne became even more pale and drawn and added to it was the tension that comes with being watched.

The fact that by summer's end Troy and Todd were following Jud like a pair of teen-age-idol worshipers didn't do much for Anne's morale either. Convinced that the twins would have capitulated just as quickly if she hadn't married Jud, Anne felt the whole thing had been an exercise in futility. Jud had given up his freedom and Lorna, and Anne could feel herself turning into a tired, frustrated shadow. And all for what? The question tormented her incessantly.

By mid-October the major part of the upheaval was over and it was obvious that Jud had made a brilliant move for the company. The employment list was up, production was up, and most important of all, everyone's morale was up.

At the end of their first almost normal week, Jud sauntered into Anne's office, stood behind her a few nervewracking seconds while he ran his eyes over the order she was working on, then calmly plucked it out of her hand and dropped it onto the desk.

"John will take care of that," he said flatly. "Get your handbag and jacket, we're leaving."

"Leaving? But why? It's only three thirty and—"

"And we have a plane to catch at six forty-five," he interrupted smoothly. "So don't argue, just move."

"I'm not moving anywhere until you tell me what this is all about." Anne retorted. "A plane to where? And why?"

"We're tired, both of us." His eyes ran over her critically. "Frankly you look like hell. We're going away for a few days, soak up some sun and rest. Mel has a house on a tiny island in the Lesser Antilles and she has offered us the use of it. I graciously accepted for the both of us."

Smarting over his remark about her looks, Anne shook her head.

"I don't want to go away with you."

His eyes narrowed and his tone went low with a silky warning.

"Want to or not you're going if I have to drag you by the hair. And if you want to pack some things, you'd better snap to it. As I said, our plane leaves in a little over three hours."

Anne bristled but pulled her desk drawer open and removed her purse. She knew better than to argue with that tone of voice.

Anne woke the following morning to the soothing sound of the ocean, the scent of lush tropical growth, and the raucous noise of brightly plumaged birds she couldn't begin to name.

The trip had been accomplished smoothly and without incident but, as it was dark when they arrived, Anne had seen very little of Melly's delightful house. She couldn't wait to explore and with an eagerness she hadn't felt in months, Anne jumped out of bed. After a quick wash she donned jeans and pull-over, then followed the mouthwatering aroma of frying bacon to the kitchen.

Whistling softly, Jud stood at the stove, alternately sipping from a cup of coffee and poking at the bacon with a long-handled fork. As she entered the room, he turned and gave her a smile that robbed her of breath.

"Good morning, wife. Your timing is perfect. If you'll set the table we can eat."

Stunned, Anne couldn't move. His easy bantering tone after weeks of strained politeness had thrown her. His taunting voice brought her to her senses.

"Wake up, little girl, and get the table ready. Unless, of course, you like your bacon burned."

His tone set the mood for the day. Together, at times hand in hand, they explored the house and grounds. Anne loved every inch of it and was only too happy to follow wherever he led her.

The house was solidly constructed to withstand the hurricanes that ripped through these islands in the fall, with a wide deck that ran completely around the single-story building. But as beautiful as the house and grounds were, the best thing about it as far as Anne was concerned was that one had only to walk down a short, gentle incline to the dazzling white sands of the beach, and thus into the unbelievably blue water.

After a very late lunch, both Anne and Jud were content to stretch out on lounge chairs on the deck and be lulled to sleep by the whisper of waves caressing the shore.

Anne woke late in the afternoon and lay quietly, allowing her eyes to roam over the sleeping form on the lounger next to hers. The last weeks had taken their toll on Jud as well as her. He looked honed down to a fine edge, not an excess ounce on his large frame, and there were new grooves cut into his face at his mouth. Fighting off the urge to reach out and smooth away those grooves, Anne slipped silently off her chair and into the house.

Fifteen minutes later, unable to resist the sun-sparkled water, Anne put on her bikini, scooped up a large bath sheet, and left the house. She dropped the huge towel on the sand and walked slowly into the water, savoring the feel as it lapped at her legs.

Some minutes later, floating on her back completely lost in her newfound, buoyant world, Anne gave a short, terrified scream when something caught and tugged at her leg. The word shark filled her mind and in blind panic she kicked her legs wildly. Her leg was released and in the next second a hard, sinewy arm slid around her waist and Jud growled in her ear.

"For God's sake, woman, relax. It's only me."

"Oh, Jud," she sputtered, "you frightened me. I thought you were a—"

The breath was knocked out of her as he pulled her against his chest and then, with a muffled curse, his mouth covered hers savagely.

With a feeling of unreality, Anne felt herself being forced down under the water. *This can't be happening,* she thought frantically. It was her nightmare all over again only now she was awake and terrified. Struggling desperately, she tore her mouth from his, heard him whisper, "Damn you, Anne," and filled her lungs with great gulps of air. Then his mouth caught hers again and she was going under—deeper, deeper.

She felt his fingers at the clasp of her bikini top and then the wisp of material was gone, lost forever in the restless waters. His hands moved with a wet

169

silkiness over her body, molding her against the hard length of him and with a low moan Anne stopped fighting.

As it had always done in her dreams, Jud's mouth drove out all fear, ignited a fire in her veins that spread rapidly through her entire body, filling her with a hungry need. In total surrender, she slipped her arms around his neck, arched her body to his and became flamingly aware that he had not bothered to put on swim trunks. She felt his hands tug at the material at her hips and then the brief panties were floating off to join their other half.

Mouths clinging, bodies entwined, they were caught up in a wave as it broke and were flung tumbling toward the beach. The force of the wave separated them and scrambling to her feet, gasping in the sweet taste of air, Anne ran out of the water and across the sand to drop choking and exhausted onto the towel.

Jud followed her slowly and watching him walk toward her, Anne's heart thumped wildly in her chest and throat. In the last rays of sunlight Jud's tall, lithe frame seemed to be cast in glowing bronze, the gold chain around his neck, with its oddly familiar egg-shaped medallion, glinting at her wickedly.

When he reached her, he stood unmoving and silent until she was forced to look up at him.

"Back there, in the water"—his voice was a ragged whisper—"you wanted me as badly as I want you. Don't turn away from me now, Anne. I need you now. I need you to be my wife."

Anne stared at him wordlessly for long seconds, then slowly raised her arms. With a low groan, he dropped to his knees beside her, pulled her into his arms and crushed her mouth with his. Within seconds

170

she was back in that fiery world his lips and hands set ablaze so effortlessly.

Gently he unlocked the door that guards all maidens, and when the pain came she heard him grunt as she unknowingly sank her teeth into his shoulder. Pleasure soon consumed all memory of pain and he grunted in an altogether different tone when she full well knowingly nipped at the other shoulder.

Later, drained of everything but the wonder of being a woman, Anne lay in Jud's arms, purring for all the world like the cat that had finally caught the canary.

When he felt her shiver from the touch of the evening air, Jud rose, scooped her up in his arms and carried her to the house. Without pausing, he went into the bathroom, adjusted the shower spray with some difficulty, and stepped into the shower with her still held firmly in his arms, all the while ignoring her squeals of protest. When the last grains of sand were sluiced away he dried, first her, then himself, then carried her to his bed, where he proceeded to teach her how to pleasure, as well as being pleasured.

Anne woke in a state of euphoria, in love with life, in love with the world and more deeply in love than ever before with the man who filled her being to the exclusion of everyone and everything else. She was alone and, wanting to rectify that, she slipped on a robe and went hunting for Jud.

She heard his voice before she reached the doorway to his uncle's small study and not wanting to disturb him she paused. A moment later she was wishing fervently she hadn't. He was speaking to John Franks and his words were like a blade, plunged into her chest.

"Yes, I know it's close on the heels of the other deal, but we can handle it. What? Oh, no problem there. She's relaxed and calm." He laughed softly. "She looks like a new woman."

Anne backed away from the doorway, fighting the urge to run. *Where could she run to?* she wept silently. There was nowhere in the world far enough.

When he found her on the deck ten minutes later, she was every inch the calm, new woman he had laughingly said she was.

"Good morning, chicken," he began as he started toward her, but the words died on his lips and his eyes narrowed as he took in her withdrawn expression.

"What's the matter, Anne?" His tone was now low, urgent. "Is it about last night? I'm sorry if I was rough at first, but—"

"There is nothing to be sorry for, Jud," she answered coldly. "I've put it from my mind, as if it never happened."

"Never happened?" he repeated in a hushed tone, then at a near shout. "Never happened? What the hell do you mean?"

"Just that, Jud." Suddenly afraid of the fury in his eyes, she turned away from him, walked several feet along the deck before turning back to him, indicating the surroundings with a wave of her hand. "I'm as human as the next, Jud. This near perfect setting," she shrugged, "I gave in to an urge." Her voice chilled scathingly. "The urge of nature. Man, woman. Male, female. Animals. Mating."

He went white and stepped back as if she'd struck him.

"Animals?" It was a hoarse groan through pale, stiff lips.

For an instant he seemed to sag with defeat, then he straightened and his eyes glittered dangerously. The old, hatefully sardonic smile twisted his mouth and he said smoothly, "Can I take it from that you are ready to go home?"

"Yes, if you don't mind."

His shrug was elegantly careless, as was his tone. "Whatever."

They returned home that night, both of them locked inside their own frozen world. The weeks that followed were the worst Anne had ever lived through. The pain and heartbreak Anne had felt when Jud went away all those years ago were nothing compared with the anguish she lived with now. And added to that anguish was a growing confusion and uncertainty, for the deal she had overheard Jud discussing with John Franks that fateful morning had not materialized.

Jud was unfailingly polite in an icy, contemptuous way and he was watching her again. She could feel his eyes on her at odd hours of the day and night, sending cold shivers down her back, raising goose bumps on her flesh. Anne wondered desperately how long she'd be able to withstand his silent assault on her nervous system.

A week after their return he strolled diffidently into her office and tossed a square white envelope onto her desk. Anne eyed it warily, saw it was addressed to Mr. and Mrs. Judson Cammeron and that it had not been opened. She didn't touch it and after a long silence he drawled sarcastically, "Your legal eagle is getting married. He requests the honor of our presence at the ceremony."

Who cares? a voice cried inside Anne, but aloud she could barely murmur, "I don't want to go."

"Too bad, because you're going to go." His eyes raked her ruthlessly. "I have already told Lorna we'd be there."

"Jud, I will not be—"

Anne sighed; she may as well have saved her breath. Jud had turned and walked back into his own office, closing the door with a final-sounding snap.

As the weeks before Andrew's late November wedding date shortened, Jud spent longer and longer periods of each week in his New York office. Anne swung widely between being sure he was being unfaithful and equally sure he was not.

Ten days before the wedding an employee problem cropped up while Jud was in New York. As the employee involved was one of executive staff and the problem was of a delicate nature, Anne, in her present mental state, felt she could not cope with it. At the dinner table that evening, Anne outlined the situation for Troy and Todd and asked them if they'd take care of it for her. Before she'd even finished speaking, they were shaking their heads emphatically.

"I wouldn't touch it with a dirty stick," Troy snorted.

"Ditto." From Todd.

With a sigh of resignation Anne left the table and went into the library. There was nothing else for her to do; she would have to telephone Jud. On the third ring the call was answered by Lorna's husky voice.

"Hello."

Anne's eyes closed slowly. Oh, God, no, she prayed. Please let there be a mistake. There was no mistake, for clear and unmistakable, as if she stood in the same room, Lorna's voice asked.

"Hello? Who is this?"

Slowly Anne lowered her arm, gently cradled the receiver. Moving like a sleepwalker, she made two more brief calls, walked out of the library, and up the stairs to her room. Twenty minutes later, suitcase in hand, she came back down the stairs and left the house.

Melly welcomed her with open arms that closed warmly and protectively around Anne's small, too slim body.

"Anne, honey, with your mother away, I'm so glad you came to me."

Margaret had left the previous week to spend a month in Florida with some friends, but even had she been home, Anne would have gone to Melly, feeling she had to get out of Jud's house.

After showing Anne to the guest room, Melly settled herself on the small, padded rocker in the room, and said bluntly, exactly as her nephew might have, "All right, let's have it. What's the problem?"

"I—I can't handle it any longer, Melly," Anne whispered. "I've made an appointment with my lawyer for next Thursday. I told him I wanted to dissolve my marriage."

Melly leaped out of her chair with the agility of a teen-ager, her face stark with shock.

"You are going to divorce Jud?"

"Yes." Anne's voice cracked, then grew stronger as she went on. "And I don't want to talk about it."

Melly opened her mouth to protest but closed it again when Anne raised her hand and said flatly. "I mean it, Mel. Unless you want me to leave right now, please don't question me."

"At least answer one question," Mell coaxed. "Does Jud know where you are? What you're planning to do?"

"No." Anne answered in the same flat tone. "And that's two questions."

"Just one more," Mell rushed on. "Do you think you're being entirely fair?"

"Fair?" Anne had to force back the hysterical laughter that rose in her throat. "Jud doesn't know the meaning of the word fair."

"Anne!"

"I'm sorry, Melly," Anne cried. "I know how much you love him and I'm truly sorry. But I won't discuss it. I can't. I'm so tired. All I want to do is rest awhile." Turning away she sobbed. "Maybe I shouldn't have come here."

"Nonsense." Melly turned her around and gave her a quick hug. "Of course you should have, and I promise you I'll ask no more questions. Now, I think you should hop into bed, start getting some of that rest you obviously do need."

In the days Anne stayed with Melly she did rest, and although she refused to talk about the action she was about to take, she did tell Melly the name of the motel she had booked a room at, when she went back.

She was packing to leave when Mel called her to the phone. Passing Mel in the hall on her way to the phone, Anne cast her a reproachful look. Shrugging fatalistically, Mel murmured.

"I only promised not to ask questions."

Lifting the phone with shaking fingers, Anne breathed, "Yes?"

"What time does your plane get in? I'll meet you."

No hello. No how are you. Just a cold, flat request for information.

"No, Jud." Anne's tone was equally cold and flat.

"Anne, we have to talk this out sometime," he argued patiently. "It may as well be tonight."

"I don't want to talk to you, Jud. My lawyer will talk for me."

"Dammit, Anne," he snapped, all pretense at patience gone. "Do you have any idea of the upheaval you've caused here? Todd and Troy have been ready to climb the walls. I was practically sitting on them to keep them from calling and upsetting your mother, when Mel called. Now stop behaving like a spoiled little girl and tell me what time your plane gets in."

She gave in and told him, thinking wearily, what difference did it make? He was right, they would have to talk sooner or later, might as well get it over with.

He was waiting at the airport, hard-faced and cold-eyed and, without a word, he retrieved her suitcase, grasped her elbow, and led her to the car.

After they were out of the worst of the traffic, Anne told him the name of the motel she wanted to go to only to have him growl.

"We're going home."

"But I don't want to go home."

"To tell you the truth, Anne," he returned tiredly, "right now I don't give one damn what you want. We can talk there without being disturbed. I shipped Troy and Todd to New York for a couple of days to work with John. We'll have the barn to ourselves." He grinned ruefully. "You can even scream at me if you want to."

Not bothering to answer him, Anne withdrew into a cold, unresponsive silence. When they reached the house, Anne flung her coat at a chair in the foyer and headed purposefully toward the living room. Jud's hand grasped her arm, pulled her around, and ignoring her struggles and protests pushed her up the stairs in front of him. When they reached her room he shoved the door open, nudged Anne inside, tossed her valise into a corner, kicked the door shut, then stood, balled fists on his hips, and demanded, "Okay, what's the story?"

The white, bulky-knit pullover he wore made his shoulders look even broader than usual and his stance, the way his eyes gleamed, frightened her. Stepping back, she moistened her dry lips.

"I'm going to divorce you, Jud. I have an appointment with my lawyer tomorrow morning."

"Why did you go away like that without a word to anyone? Why didn't you at least let me know where you were."

His harsh voice flung the questions at her like stones and in a tone of equal harshness she flung the answer back.

"Because I didn't want you to know where I was. I didn't want to see you or talk to you."

Turning around, she walked to the window, stared at her own reflection.

"I still don't."

"Are you trying to kill me by inches?"

Barely breathing, Anne stood perfectly still. His voice had dropped to a ragged whisper and his words threw her off balance. Beginning to tremble, she turned to look at him.

"What are you talking about?"

"You, and the hell you've put me through," he lashed out at her. "I was damn near out of my mind when Mel called me."

"But why?" she cried out in bewilderment. "Jud, I don't understand you."

"Don't you?" he rasped. "Well, then, maybe it's time you did."

Had he gone mad? Eyes widening, Anne watched as his hands yanked the sweater, tugged it up his body and over his head. With a violent motion he threw it down, then lifted his head to stare at her.

"Come here, Anne."

Half afraid to move, more afraid not to, she walked unsteadily across the room, coming to a stop in front of him.

"The medal I wear on the chain. Does it look familiar, Anne?"

Anne's eyes dropped to the oddly shaped medal, then, a look of disbelief on her face, they flew back to his.

"Take it in your hand. Examine it closely."

Her eyes went back to the medal as hesitantly, fingers shaking, she touched it, lifted it from his chest. The oval was warm from the touch of his skin, its mat finish glittering dully in the artificial light and etched onto its surface were the initials J. C. C. Turning it over, she saw the back was exactly the same, etched with the same initials.

She had no need to speak, her eyes asked the question.

"I never wore them as links," he said quietly.

Her finger moved over the surface.

"But how? Why?"

"How? Very simple." His hands came up to cover hers, closing it around the disc. "Not long after I left, I took it to a jeweler, he removed the posts, fused the two together and attached the loop. I've worn it ever since. It's been my talismen, my good luck charm, my curse. Except when I went into surgery when my nose was broken, I've never had it off. Why? Because it was all I had of you."

The pain in his voice tore at Anne's heart. What was he trying to do to her? Jerking her hand from his, she stepped back.

"But you went away," she sobbed, "You went away."

"You drove me away."

Shocked by his suddenly renewed anger, she stood dumbly, shaking her head.

"Why did you come to my room that night, Anne? Were you experimenting? Were you curious?" His harsh voice hammered at her. Giving her no time to deny his words, he went on. "Do you have any idea what it does to a twenty-five-year-old man to face the fact that he's in love with a fifteen-year-old girl? Or what it's like to watch that girl grow into a lovely young woman? Wanting her? Needing her?"

"But there were other women, Jud," Anne cried hopelessly. "I know there were."

"Hell, yes," he shot back. "There were a lot of women before that night. And a lot more since. And for the same reason. Always the same reason. To exorcise you."

Reaching out his arm, he caught hers, drew her close to him.

"And you know what?" His voice was a tormented groan. "It didn't work. I said I'll always love you and I always have. Even while I was hating you I loved you, so no matter what you do, I guess I always will. I don't want to, Anne, but I do. And I'm not going to let you divorce me."

Anne closed her eyes, afraid to breathe, afraid to move, afraid that if she did she'd hear him laugh and say he was lying and she knew she could not bear that.

"Anne?"

The note of hesitant fear that laced Jud's tone set off a million tiny lights inside Anne, and not pausing to think she whispered, "Oh, Jud. I love you so much I can't stand it."

For one terrifying second he didn't move, and then she was hauled roughly against him and held there tightly in hard, possessive arms. Murmuring her name, he bent his head but she lifted her hand to put her fingers over his lips. She knew the mindless state his kiss could induce. She had to have some answers first.

"Jud, no."

He stiffened then leaned back, his arms loosening.

180

"No? Anne what are you trying to do to me?"

"Jud, I'm sorry, but I must know. How did I drive you away? Was I too young? Too inexperienced?"

His hand came up to cradle her face, hold it still. Bending his head, he dropped a light, tantalizing kiss on her mouth and murmured, "Of course you were too young. But I was past worrying about age at that point and, if you hadn't told him you never wanted to see me again, nothing would have kept me away from you."

"Your father?" Anne's eyes flew wide.

"Yes," he sighed. "My father. We had one hell of a fight. Even after he told me how you begged him to send you away so you wouldn't have to see me again, I insisted on seeing you. He was determined I wouldn't. I came pretty close to hitting him that night, Anne. I loved him. Hell, I damned near idolized him, but I came very, very close. We were shouting at each other. I had never seen him so mad."

Dropping his hands, he moved away from her. She saw a shudder ripple across his naked shoulders and when he turned to face her again, his eyes were bleak, his face pale, ravaged with memories.

He went on the prowl, moving restlessly around the room, fingers raking through his hair.

"He called me all kinds of names, none of them pretty. He accused me of trying to rape you. Told me that I had probably scarred you for life. By then I must have seemed like someone demented. I told him I had to see you, tell you." He stopped pacing, shot her a hard look. "He kept repeating how you'd begged him to keep me away from you. Said that if I had an ounce of decency I'd get out and stay out. By the time I left, he had me feeling like I should crawl instead of walk."

Tears running down her face, Anne sobbed. "I didn't say anything. He gave me some pills, I fell asleep. The next morning—when I woke up—I—I kept thinking, everything will be all right, Jud will make it all right. And then, when I found out you were gone— Oh, Jud, I was so sure you'd come for me. I waited and waited."

Jud went absolutely still at her words, the raw pain in her voice. Growing pale under the burnished tan, his face revealed the conflict of emotions he was feeling. Lids that had gone wide now narrowed over eyes that combed her face, searched for truth. He found it in the eyes that pleaded to be believed, the anguish in the one word she whispered.

"Jud."

His face twisted with inner torment and his eyes closed completely as he expelled a long, ragged sigh. In three strides he was across the room. Pulling her into his arms he pressed her face against his rough chest.

"Damn him," he snarled. "Damn him to the same hell he put me through."

"Jud! You mustn't say that," she cried wildly. "He probably thought he was protecting me."

"He damned near protected you into marriage with Andrew." A shudder rippled through his body and his arms tightened possessively. "I came so close to losing you," his voice dropped to a hoarse growl. "Damn him."

"Jud, don't," Anne sobbed. "He's gone. Please, please don't hate anymore."

"Okay, okay," he murmured. "I'm sorry. Calm down."

His hand at the back of her head lifted her face to meet his searching mouth and in between short, hungry kisses he murmured, "Don't cry, chicken. I promise you, we'll make up for all those years."

"What about Lorna?"

"Lorna?" An expression of total blankness crossed his face. "What about her? She's marrying Andrew tomorrow."

"I—I thought you were in love with her. That you'd given her up and married me, to get control of the firm."

"Good God!" His arms tightened, his lips teased hers. "I married you to get control of you. Say the word and I'll go to the phone, transfer my shares to Troy and Todd, if you'll call and cancel your appointment with your lawyer."

"You know I'm going to cancel that appointment," she admitted, "as well as you know I'd never ask you to give up your shares."

His soft laughter did strange things to Anne's spine. It was a lighthearted, teasing sound. A sound she had not heard in over ten years.

"I know," he grinned, then he sobered again. "But I would do it, honey. I'd do just about anything to keep you with me."

While his one hand caressed the back of her head, the other moved sensuously over her back, drawing her closer, closer to his body.

"Oh, Anne," he groaned, "even when I hated you the most, I wanted you. There were times when I thought I'd go crazy with wanting you. When I first heard that rumor about you and the old man—" He closed his eyes a moment and when he opened them again they were blazing with remembered fury. "I wanted to kill you—both of you. I spent the last few years before I came home hating you. Or believing I did. When I stood in that cemetery and stared at his coffin, I knew I had been lying to myself. I loved him."

"You were at the cemetery?"

"Yes, I was at the cemetery." He cocked a pale brow at her in self-mockery. "And when I walked into the library afterward, I knew nothing had changed for me. I still loved you, I still wanted you, and I still thought of you as mine. As for Lorna, she is a good secretary and a good friend and nothing more."

"Then why did she answer the phone in your apartment the day I called?" The strident note of jealousy in her own voice startled Anne and she caught her lip between her teeth.

"What day?" The sharpness of his tone conflicted with the genuine bafflement in his eyes.

"The day I left to go to Melly's," Anne whispered, suddenly not sure she wanted to hear the reason Lorna was there. "I called the apartment because of a problem at the mill I didn't know how to handle," she explained hurriedly. "When Lorna answered, I hung up."

"Having jumped to the obvious, but incorrect, conclusion." Jud's arms tightened around her as he lowered his head, rubbed his cheek against her hair. "If you hadn't hung up, you'd have learned there were several people with me that night, including Lorna's father. We were having an informal, if serious, business meeting over dinner. Lorna was there as my secretary, nothing more." He sighed, drew his head back to look at her, a teasing light entering his eyes. "Although I must admit that a few times I deliberately used Lorna's name in the hope of getting a reaction from you." His arms tightened even more, almost painfully. "I was so damned jealous of Andrew and I

184

wanted you to feel something, if only a tiny measure, of the pain I was in."

"But there was no reason to be jealous of Andrew," Anne exclaimed. "Not ever."

"Now she tells me," Jud murmured ruefully.

By now his hand was on her hip, pressing her tightly against him. His blatant need ignited an answering one in her. Lightheaded with happiness, starving for his love, she ran her hands up and over his chest, fingers sliding through the dark-gold hair.

"My legs are getting very tired standing here, Jud," she whispered. "Couldn't we find a more comfortable place to talk?"

His soft laughter rippled over her again and he gave her a swift, hard kiss before swinging her off her feet into his arms. "Yes, but not here." Carrying her effortlessly he went through the connecting bathroom into his bedroom. Standing her on her feet beside his bed, he stared into her eyes a long moment, the amber of his eyes seeming to glow like hot, melted honey. Then, his hands gentle, trembling slightly, he sensuously undressed her. Still moving slowly, as if savoring every minute, he eased her back onto the bed, caught her wrists in one hand and pulled her arms taut over her head.

"I had to see you like this. I had to." Jud's voice was raw with hunger, his eyes molten as they burned over her. "For almost eleven years my mind carried a picture of you stretched out across my bed. At times that picture damned near drove me mad."

"Oh, Jud." The two whispered words were all Anne could force out of her emotion-clogged throat. Desire, hot and fierce, clamored through her body and she thought that if he didn't kiss her soon, touch her, she'd go out of her mind.

"The reality puts the picture to shame." His soft,

185

hoarse voice was a seduction in itself and Anne's body moved with the tremor that rippled through her. She heard his sharply indrawn breath before he lowered his head, brought his mouth close to hers, whispered. "Part your lips for me, Anne."

The gentle touch of his mouth on hers was a covenant, a seal, a blessing that quickly changed to an urgent, fiery demand. He did not make love to her. He had made love to her while they had been on the island. Now, he worshiped her. With his hands, his mouth, his entire body, he worshiped her.

His mouth left a trail of fire from her throbbing lips to her aching breasts, wrenched a gasp of pleasure from her with his teasing, tormenting tongue. His stroking hands sent shivers chasing each other in a tingling cascade to the base of her spine, drew a longing moan from deep in her throat when they caressingly feathered the inside of her thighs. His hard, muscular body, tawny hide warm under her fingers, moved against her with maddening slowness until, her hands gripping his hips, she drew him to her with a sobbing outcry.

"Jud, please, please love me."

He did. Long into the night, stripping away all inhibitions, all shyness, he brought her to full womanhood, fulfilled and fulfilling.

When Anne opened her eyes, the room was bright with sunshine from outside and Jud's eyes, lazily studying her face, were bright with a light from within.

"I love you." No frills, no curlicues, his voice held a steady, truthful ring.

"I don't love you." Anne turned her head, pressed her lips to his throat.

"No?" Jud drawled indulgently.

186

"No. I adore you, I worship you, I—"

"Enough," he laughed softly, lowering his head to brush his lips across her temple. "I'll settle for that."

His arms drew her close, tightening in a fierce bear hug, before he released her completely and sprang out of bed. Throwing his head back, he lifted his arms high over his head to stretch luxuriously like a large contented cat.

Her eyes moving slowly over his beautiful body, Anne was surprised, after the loving night she'd been through, at the growing ache deep in her body, the tingling arousal of her nipples.

"God, I feel good," he joyfully told the ceiling, then his head swung down and around, eyes fastening on her bemused, smiling face. "Rustle that enticing tush, woman," he ordered. "We have places to go. Things to do."

"Where do we have to go?" Startled out of her erotic musings, Anne flushed pink. "What do we have to do?"

Moving around the room restlessly, totally unconcerned with his nakedness, Jud said, "First we are going to call your mother, Troy, and Todd, tell them to stay away at least two more weeks." White teeth flashed in a quick grin. "I may even set their minds at rest by assuring them that I really do love you. After that I'm going to take you for something to eat before we go shopping for a wedding gift. We were invited to a wedding today, you know."

"You really want to go to that wedding?" Anne asked in astonishment.

"I'm afraid we slept through the wedding, honey." Happy laughter rippled from his throat. "But, yes, I want to go to the reception. After we've chosen a suitable gift I'm going to shop for you, buy you the most fantastic gown we can find." His eyes lit with deviltry. "Then I'm going to escort you to that damned reception and watch every man there eat his heart out, because you belong to me."

"Jud, you're crazy," Anne laughed. "Now tell me the real reason you want to go."

"Because I want to celebrate," he grinned. "And Andrew and Lorna's party is as good a place as any. Besides, all our friends have been concerned about you. It will please them to see the completely satisfied look you're wearing."

"Completely satisfied?"

Letting the sheet slip from her, Anne sat up slowly. Doing her own impression of a stretching feline, she felt her breasts rise tautly, hardened tips point at him. Through her lashes she watched his eyes narrow, the instant response of his body.

"The hell with it," Jud purred, moving toward the bed. "We'll mail the gift."

With a delighted squeal Anne moved to get up. Jud's diving body pinned her to the bed. His lips moved against hers. "We can call the family later. Much later."

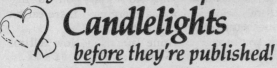